Tom Clancy's
Net Force Explorers:
The Deadliest Game

Created by Tom Clancy and Steve Pieczenik

HEADLINE
FEATURE

First published in Great Britain in 1998
by HEADLINE BOOK PUBLISHING

A HEADLINE FEATURE paperback

10 9 8 7 6 5 4 3

ISBN 0 7472 6070 2

Typeset by
Letterpart Limited, Reigate, Surrey

Printed and bound in Great Britain by
Caledonian International Book Manufacturing Ltd, Glasgow

HEADLINE BOOK PUBLISHING
A division of Hodder Headline PLC
338 Euston Road
London NW1 3BH

Acknowledgments

We'd like to thank the following people, without whom this book would not have been possible: Diane Duane, for help in rounding out the manuscript; Martin H. Greenberg, Larry Segriff, Denise Little, and John Helfers at Tekno Books; Mitchell Rubenstein and Laurie Silvers at BIG Entertainment; Tom Colgan, of Putnam Books; Robert Youdelman, Esquire, and Tom Mallon, Esquire; and Robert Gottlieb of the William Morris Agency, agent and friend. We much appreciated the help.

Prologue

It was the kind of windowless room found in any one of a thousand office buildings nowadays, since the world had become truly virtual and any wall could become a window at the will of the inhabitants. However, the inhabitants of this particular room seemed unwilling to indulge even the illusion of windowing: or perhaps what they disliked was the basic implication of a window, that someone might be able to see in as well as out. The walls were blind and bare, though they glowed softly white, shedding a cool even light over the large, shiny black table in the middle of the room, and over the five men sitting at one end of it.

They were Suits. Some of their lapels or ties were marginally slenderer than others, or wider: only those slight cues to their ages or preferences in fashion made them look at all different from one another. Otherwise, their ties were all subdued, and their shirts were plain white or pale colors, no prints. In nearly all ways they were unremarkable-looking men, and wore

1

that unremarkableness like a disguise.

It was one.

'So when will it be ready?' said the one who sat at the center of the group.

'It's ready now,' said the man sitting furthest from him on his left, a youngish-looking man with iron-colored hair and iron-grey eyes. 'The controls have been in place for eighteen months now, consolidating their positions and getting ready to go into maximal intervention mode.'

'And no one suspects?'

'No one. We've had zero tolerance for leaks . . . not that it would have been that much of a problem *had* there been one. The environment is so intrinsically chaotic that you could drop a tactical nuke in it and get a lot of hair-tearing and recriminations, but absolutely no profitable analysis.' The youngish man laughed a scornful one-breath laugh. 'No one there is interested in analysis, anyway: the context is completely devoted to raw sensation and "experience." Even when the program starts running, no one will have the slightest idea what's going on until everything's over and it's much too late.'

The man in the center turned to one of the two on his right, an older man with a deeply lined face and shaggy blond hair going silver. 'What about the people at Ecs? Are they set?'

The man with the silver-gilt hair nodded. 'They had the point of maximum economic result picked several months ago. All the projections have matched 'real-world' outcomes . . . if 'real' is the word we're looking for. We can move the world, all right. The lever's ready. All we need to do now is pick the place to stand.'

The man in the center nodded. 'All right. Your two sections will need to work very closely together on this, but you have been anyway. Make sure you pick the right "spot" . . . and when you start to push, don't spare the effort: I want the whole thing overturned. A lot of people are watching this demonstration, and they'll expect to see something spectacular for all the funds they've diverted – excuse me, "laterally invested"–' and the others smiled – 'toward setting up the best possible result. Make absolutely certain the endgame position matches the modeling. I don't want any bull afterwards about "equivocal results".'

The two men to whom he had spoken nodded.

'All right,' said the man in the center. 'Lunch with the people from Tokagawa is at one-thirty. Don't be late: we want to make a unified presentation, and you know what a stickler that miserable little old man is for manners.'

'If this works out,' said one of the men to whom he had not spoken, 'we won't need to mind our manners much longer. *He'll* be the one who'll have to be looking over his shoulder.'

The man in the center looked at him: a slow, deliberate turn of the head, like a targeting mechanism turning on gimbals and locking on.

'If?' he said.

The other man went slightly pale, and glanced down at the table.

The man in the center held the look for a few

seconds more, then stood. The others stood with him. 'The car will be here at five after one,' he said. 'Let's get on with it.'

The man who had gone pale was first out of the room, closely followed by the only one who had not spoken. The young iron-haired man glanced at the man in the center, then followed the others out. The door shut.

Then the man in the middle chuckled softly. 'A nuke, huh?' he said. 'It might be funny.'

The man with the silver-gilt hair produced a slightly sardonic expression, and turned to follow in the wake of the others. 'Well,' he said, 'frankly, I don't know if I'd bother. They'd probably just think it was magic . . .'

Chapter 1

Fords of Ariel, Talairn, Virtual Dominion of Sarxos:
Greenmonth 13, Year of the Dragon-In-The-Rain

The place smelled like a breakdown at a sewage treatment facility. That was what Shel most noticed as he pushed aside the tent's doorflap and gazed out into the fading sunset light.

He looked out wearily over the russet-lit, shadow-streaked vista of pine woods and sloping fields and riverbanks which had become, at about noon today, a battlefield. Then, for a few magic minutes, it had been exactly what one's dreams of such a place would be at their best. There were the armies drawn up in their serried ranks, spears glinting and banners snapping bright in the brisk wind and the sun, and the trumpets shouting brazen defiance across the river which had been the boundary between their two forces, his and Delmond's. Delmond had come marching down the road to the river with his two thousand horse and three thousand foot, and had sent his herald Azure Alaunt over the water with the usual defiance, or rather the defiance that had become typical of Delmond as he pushed his way across Sarxos's lesser kingdoms. There were none of the courtesies which one opposing commander usually paid the other – no offer of single combat to spare the armies the bloodshed which must follow: not even the commonplace and pragmatic suggestion that the two armies' quartermasters meet to investigate the possibility of one side buying out the contracts of the other army's mercenaries, a move which would often render a battle unnecessary if as a result the strength of one side suddenly doubled and the other's was halved. No, Delmond wanted to take Shel's little land of Talairn on the other side of the Artel; and more, he wanted a fight – wanted the smell of blood in the afternoon, and the sound of trumpets.

So Shel let him have it.

There was no use pretending it hadn't been satisfying. Delmond's tactics had been positively insulting – no scouts, no attempt to reconnoiter or secure the battlesite ahead of time. He'd simply marched right up the North Road to the River Artel as if there had been nothing to fear, and after that brief pause to issue formal defiance to the troops drawn up on the other side, Delmond had forded the Artel at the head of his forces, heading straight up the gentle grassy rise on the far side of the river as if there was absolutely no cause to be concerned about attacking uphill, and into cavalry already emplaced. Delmond was heading for Minsar, the little city about two miles up the road from the fords of the Artel. He had apparently decided that the mixed force of five hundred cavalry and two thousand foot which Shel had positioned between the river and the road to Minsar was an obstacle easily swept aside: more so because, to judge by the lack of differencing pennons on the great banner of the Talairn forces, Shel was apparently not with them.

But the Artel was an old river, winding and deeply oxbowed among the gentle pine-clad hills through which it meandered. Those hills held many secrets for the knowledgeable wanderer. Many little tracks and hidden roads, hunters' paths and game paths wound among and over them as the river wound around . . . and the paths and tracks were all quite hidden under the thick boughs or the towering pines and firs. The ground under those big old trees was cushioned deep with old dry needles that would muffle the sound of anything that moved.

So it was that, when Delmond's forces were halfway across the river – the cavalry first, the foot following, and the cavalry beginning almost casually to engage the Talairn cavalry uphill – they had been taken completely by surprise as Shel and eight hundred of his picked horsemen came plunging down from the surrounding hills on both sides of the river, and took both Delmond's horse and foot in their flanks. Delmond's cavalry, boxed in on the Minsar side of the river or still trying to flounder their way out of the water, were driven down into the mud and reeds and sedges to either side of the ford, and slaughtered there by Shel's halberd-armed foot. Delmond's infantry, predictably and sensibly, tried to run away, but there wasn't much of anywhere for them to run *to*. The Talairn cavalry, with Shel leading one of the four forces which had come plunging down from the shelter of the pines, surrounded them and began chopping them down like some bloody harvest. Within a very short time, the battle was over.

Put like that, it sounded simple: but there had been nothing simple about it. Any true account of the battle would have to include the hours and hours, starting before dawn that morning, that Shel had spent getting his mounted troops in place up on the hills, every move being made in strictly enforced silence while he prayed that the early mist off the river would not lift until all his people were under cover. Mention would have to be made of the dead chill under the pines, early on, in which breath smoked and teeth chattered – followed in only a couple of hours by the stifling heat of an unseasonably warm, breathless spring day: the bug bites, the maddening itch of pine needles down Shel's tunic and under his chainmail as he crept from position to position, making sure his people were where they needed to be, cheering them up with a well-placed word of encouragement here and there, when it was *he* who needed the encouragement, but dared not show it. The description would have to include the lance of pure fear that struck straight through him as he heard the sassy brass challenge of Delmond's trumpets coming down the road on the far side of the river, approaching the ford. Anticipation mixed with utter dread that even now Delmond might think to send some scouts up into the pines – but then came the flush of combined relief and absolute rage as Delmond did no such thing. *Thank Rod for small favors*, Shel thought, and a second later, furious, thought, *What the hell kind of general does he take me for? I'll show the sonofa—*

—and then one last dreadful thrill of fear as Delmond's forces forded the river, still playing their blaring trumpets. *What do they think this is, a Memorial Day parade? . . . We'll see who needs a memorial in a couple of hours!* – and they made their way up the far side of the ford, toward his troops, waiting there: his troops, under his eager young lieutenant Alla, who had no orders except *Don't let them past. Hang on!*

They hung on. It was very close. They had to stay there without relief, and fight on their own, long enough to make sure that Delmond's whole cavalry force took the bait and crossed the river to the unfavorable uphill ground. If any of them lingered on the far bank of the river, all Shel's carefully planned tactics would have gone straight to hell. But his enemy's fighting psychology was all too plain at this point in time. A few victories against careless or unlucky adversaries had convinced Delmond of his skill as a strategist and tactician; though Shel knew Delmond had little real skill in either art. All it needed now was the obvious opening, for a seemingly easy win, to tempt Delmond into the obvious move. Delmond took it . . . and even then Shel had to suffer through many minutes of torment and uncertainty while his little force on the far side of the river stood their ground and met Delmond's first charge—

Then, along with his picked horsemen, *then* Shel had

been able to vault into the saddle and blow his horn for the signal to charge, and had led his riders whooping down the hillsides in a crash of hooves and dislodged stones, taking Delmond's infantry at open shields from left and right, and his split cavalry force from behind and both sides. The cry of 'A Shel! A Shel!' had gone up from his forces on the Minsar side of the river, their desperation turned to rage and triumph in a moment, and they began cutting their way toward him as he and his horsemen cut toward them—

The worst of it had really been over about half an hour later, though the cleanup, as usual, took until sunset . . . not that anything was much cleaner at the end of it all. Survivors were herded together and disarmed, as many of them as could be found: wounded fighters had to be picked up and brought in; the ransomable, those of them who could be located after attempting to make themselves unrecognizable, had to be separated out, their worth determined, sureties taken from them and parole given. Shel had had to supervise it all, getting tireder and tireder by the moment.

And now it was all finished, except for the most important part, the reason the whole battle had happened in the first place: dealing with Delmond. Shel had truly not thought this far ahead, and he was still surprised that Delmond had fallen for his tactics at all. But then the Swiss had been surprised, too, when the Austrians had fallen for a variation on this theme at Morgarten. Delmond had never been much of a reader, though, and was therefore condemned to repeat the great military mistakes of earlier centuries. Shel, for his own part, thought it served Delmond right.

Outside, the trumpets were blowing a tired version of the *recheat*, signaling that pickup had been made on all the wounded, and it was now safe for noncombatants, the husbands and wives of the fallen who might have been following either force, to reclaim the bodies of their relatives. Shel took one last look at the battlefield, which was becoming more and more deeply drowned in rose-tinged, foggy shadow as the mist rose off the River Artel and crept over the ground, mercifully hiding what still lay there. After a moment he let the tentflap fall, and went to sit down in the camp chair by his map table, letting out a long, weary breath.

When he had fought his first battle in Sarxos, a few years ago, Shel had come equipped with the usual images of how the aftermath of a mighty battle ought to look: his standard flying bravely over the stricken field, and the standard of his enemy thrown down in the dust. Now, with a little more experience behind him, numerous battles lost and won, he knew that there was precious little dust to be found on one of *these* battlefields. This morning, in the sunshine, the slight slope leading up from the fords had been a great sheep-cropped expanse of green grass, all speckled with white daisies and the small yellow blossoms of nevermind. Now, after the trampling of twenty thousand hooves and ten thousand feet, it was mud. *Red* mud – it stuck to your boots with horrible tenacity. His enemy's standard, trampled well into it, would now be just one more sodden rag, indistinguishable from any-body's collapsed tent, or from some petty noble's sur-coat flung off to keep its owner from being captured and held for a fat ransom. As for the stricken field, it was Shel who always felt stricken, the next morning, at the smell. Nor was it any wonder that the husbands and wives and other relatives of the fallen always showed up as soon as the battle was over, or any time well before dawn, to ask permission to search for the bodies of their loved ones. They knew, from too much painful experi-ence, what the place would smell like once the sun was up and had had a chance to warm things.

Shel intended to be well away from here by then. His tent was already unable to keep out the battlefield stink of stamped-out guts – or of guts not lost, but just loose, the results of many a brave young warrior's first encounter with the battlefield. *War is hell*, went the saying. But at the moment, Shel felt more inclined to substitute another four-letter word for 'hell:' certainly he would have preferred the smell of brimstone to the aroma most prevalent just now.

'It's only a game,' he told himself . . . and then made a face. The game's creator, a careful and thorough craftsman, had done his job too well for such bland assurances to make a difference: no action was permit-ted to evade its consequences. The air should have been sweet with the oncoming evening, and wasn't. There would of course be a great celebration of Shel's victory later, when he got back to Minsar, a mighty meeting to congratulate the heroes who had contrib-uted to the win, and there the banners would fly and the trumpets would sing, and the bards would chant their praises . . . but not here. This place could be cleaned up by no lesser force than Nature, and even she would take some months about it. Even after the grass was green again and the daisies bloomed, the sheep which grazed these pastures would be working around swords and arrowheads and the stained bones and skulls for quite a few years.

At least the grass would be of high quality, and lush, come the later summer. Blood was an extraordinary fertilizer . . .

The tentflap lifted: one of Shel's guardsmen looked in, an old companion called Talch. Shel glanced up at him.

'When do you want to see him, sir?' said Talch. He was a big man, cavalry, still all spattered from today's work, with mud and blood and Rod knew what else: he stank, but then so did Shel, and so did everyone else for a mile around.

'Twenty minutes or so,' said Shel, reaching across the map table for a pitcher of honeydraft. 'Let me do something about my blood sugar first. Has he said anything?'

'Not a word.'

Shel raised his eyebrows, encouraged. Delmond was known for his tendency to brag even when he had lost, as long as he thought he had a chance of getting out of a situation. 'Good. Have you had anything to eat?'

'Not yet. Nick's been out hunting. Got a deer – they're butchering it. But no one wants to eat here, really . . .'

'Why would they? And we won't, either. Send some-one up toward Minsar to start some cooking fires outside the walls: we'll encamp there tonight. And tell Alla I'll hear her report now.'

Talch nodded, let the tentflap fall. Shel looked at it and wondered, as he sometimes did, whether Talch was a player or a construct, one of many 'extra' personnel whom the game itself contained. There were plenty of them, since most people preferred to play more interesting characters than guards and camp-followers; though you never could tell. One of the greatest generals of the twenty-two-year run of Sarxos, the cavalry-master Alainde, had spent nearly two years playing a laundryman in the service of Grand Duke Erbin before beginning his startling rise through the ranks. At any rate, in the etiquette of Sarxos, 'are you a player?' was not a question you ever asked. It 'broke the spell.' If a player chose to come out to *you*, that was different, and afterwards you thanked him for his trust. But there were tens of thousands of players in Sarxos who preferred to remain anonymous as to both their names and their status, people who might dip into the Virtual Domain for an evening's enjoyment every now and then, or who might come in night after night, as Shel did, in pursuit of something specific – amuse-ment, excitement, adventure, revenge, power – or just escape from a real world whose reality sometimes became just a little too grinding.

Shel took a long drink of the honeydraft, and sat and thought, pausing a moment to shake himself, and scratch: more pine needles down his tunic . . . it would be days before they were all gone. He would really have preferred to do the rest of this evening's work in the morning, but there was no telling what kind of trickery Delmond might attempt to pull if he were allowed the time. Even in his present strong position, Shel couldn't ignore Delmond's slippery reputation. His mother, Tarasp of the Hills, was a wizard-lordling, one notoriously nonaligned, who shifted stances between Light and Dark without warning. From her Delmond had inherited both some small measure of power as a shapeshifter, and a dangerous shiftiness of temperament which made him capable of signing a peace treaty with one hand while holding, spell-concealed in the other, the knife intended for your guts. Once he had actually attempted such an assassination in the tent where he was supposed to be coming to terms with someone else who had beaten him in battle. There were people in the game who admired this kind of tactic, but Shel didn't think much of it, and had no intention of falling foul of it now.

In the meantime, Shel wasn't too worried about the success of any assassination attempt on *him*. Leaning against the tentpole, unsheathed, was his hand-and-a-half broadsword: a very simple-looking implement, gray steel with a slight blue sheen. It had many names, but then most swords in Sarxos did – the ones that were worth anything, anyway. The sword which people around here called Ululator (or Howler) had a nasty reputation, and was well known for its ability to protect its master without him having to actually handle it. Few heard Ululator's scream and lived to tell about it.

15

Shel cocked his head at the sound of footsteps outside, and the sound of complaints, and then emphatic swearing, in Elstern.

'Talch?'

A pause, and his guard stuck his head into the tent.

'Our boy getting impatient out there?'

His guard produced a sardonic grin and said, 'Seems his dignity's injured because we haven't given him his own tent.'

'He should count himself lucky his dignity's all that's injured.'

'I think most of the camp would agree. Meanwhile, sir, Alla's waiting, when you're ready to start.'

'Ask her to come in.'

'Right, sir.'

The tentflap fell, then was tossed aside again. Alla came in, her mail ringing softly over her long deerskin tunic as she moved, and Shel's heart bounced, as it had done for a while now when he looked at her after a fight. She was a Valkyrie – not literally, but in body type: big, strong but not overmuscled, and dazzlingly blond, with a face that could go from friendly to feral in a matter of seconds . . . which it did, on the battle-field. She was another of the people about whom Shel was most curious in Sarxos: was she real on both sides of the interface, or just this one? Again, he wouldn't ask, but in Alla's case, Shel's reticence had just a little more to do with nervousness than etiquette. He would have been unhappy to find that there was no Alla in the real world: and to find that there *was* one would immediately have raised the question, *And what are you going to do about it?* For the time being, he left well alone. *But someday,* he thought, *someday I'm going to find a way to work around to the subject myself . . . ever so gradually. And if she wants to say anything, well . . .*

'How are you feeling?' Shel said. 'Did you see the barber?'

She sat down, making a face which suggested she didn't much see the need. 'Yes . . . he stitched the leg up all right. Didn't take long: he says it'll be healed tomorrow – he put one of those sustained-release spells on it. How about you? Got the shakes out of your system yet?'

'Please,' said Shel. 'It'll be a week or more. I hate battles.'

Alla rolled her eyes expressively. 'You must . . . you have so many of them. You want the accounting now?'

'Yes.'

'Of our forces: one hundred and ninety-six dead, three hundred and forty wounded, twelve of those critical. Of Delmond's: two thousand and fourteen dead, a hundred and sixty-odd wounded, forty critical.'

Shel whistled softly. The news of this spectacular success would spread: it might keep some of the more land-hungry or fight-hungry denizens of Sarxos's south continent out of his hair for a while. Many would think superior strategy had been involved. Even more would think it had been magic . . . which suited Shel. 'Other captives?'

'Thirty unwounded infantry captives. Not a lot of unhurt nobles, maybe ten: almost all the rest of them are wounded, or went down fighting. Everybody else not accounted for seems to have run away, southward mostly.'

'Back to his cities . . . What's the matter with these people? Do they *like* being cavalry fodder?'

Alla shrugged. She was not overly political: her preferences ran to fighting and eating, though what she did with the calories was an eternal mystery to Shel, and a cause for some envy. If he even looked sideways at a meat pie or a haunch of roast boar, he gained weight. 'Anything else?' Shel said.

'You might want to look at the contents of their baggage train,' Alla said, pulling a piece of parchment out of her tunic and handing it to him.

Shel scanned down it, and as he read, his mouth dropped open. 'What the— What did he need all *this* stuff for?'

'Seems there was going to be a big victory party in Minsar tonight,' Alla said, stretching lazily, but her face was wearing that feral look. 'Fancy clothes and fancy food and an exhibition of rich booty for the victors: ritual humiliation for the losers . . . the usual thing. Nooses around our necks, people pelting us with beef bones and pig knuckles.'

Shel snorted. 'As if they were likely to find any . . . this is sheep country.'

'Yeah, well. Instead of his big victory dinner and massive boozefest, and instead of all the other local rulers getting very nervous, now Delmond gets the scraps, and *we* get his baggage train.'

Shel nodded, though he was still incredulously reading the baggage manifest. 'The absolute stupidity of bringing all this stuff along . . . I can't *believe* he's this naive . . . he must be up to something. I wonder: who has Delmond been dealing with lately that it would be to his advantage to make them think he's stupid, or mad?'

Alla raised her eyebrows. 'Us?'

Shel glanced at her. 'You suggesting that he threw us this battle on purpose? Walked into the trap despite expecting it to be there?'

'He doesn't care much about his people's lives, if that's the case,' Alla said. 'But that wouldn't be news.'

'Hmm.' Shel sat there for a moment, thinking about it. 'Well, we'll see. If it *wasn't* us he was trying to fool . . .' He sat back, thinking which of his recent opponents might have been behind Delmond's actions somehow: who would it benefit? *Argath maybe? Not him . . . he's usually a little more straightforward than this. Elblai? . . . no, she's getting ready to square off with Argath, last I heard . . . some attempt to undermine the Tripartite Alliance?* Shel thought about that, letting his mind range briefly among the possibilities, and his eyes strayed to something else on his map table, a rolled-up piece of parchment which had been lying there quietly smoking. Alliances were shifting all over Sarxos at the moment, as the Dark Lord began his nine-yearly movement out of his mountain-bordered land, seeking the final conquest of all the lands of the Dominion. Every time he tried this, the Sarxonian lords united to throw him back: but the last union had been a little less organized than usual, the alliance taking almost too long to come together . . . and the Dark Lord had begun his next round of 'diplomatic initiatives' much sooner than usual after his defeat. Almost as if he thought this time he might actually win . . .

It was complicated, but then most things in Sarxos were: that was what made playing the game worthwhile. Meanwhile, Shel would have to handle Delmond in such a manner as not to bring the man's enemies down on his back right away – especially his mother, who was a power in the Dominion in her own right, with many potentially troublesome connections – but also in some way which would seem fair, possibly even make him look good.

'I think you should kill him,' Alla said.

Shel gave her a slight, sidelong smile. 'Not enough points in it,' he said, but that was not the real reason, and he knew Alla knew it. She rolled her eyes again.

'He's a waste of your time,' Alla said.

'If one would be Lord of All the Wide Dominion some day,' Shel said, 'one has to behave properly at the start of the game, as well as the finish. Let's just call this practice, shall we? Anything else I need to know about the cleanup?'

Alla shook her head. 'Quartermaster wants to know when we'll be converting all this junk into money. The troops are getting a little, well, restive at being so close to so much gold.'

'I just bet. We'll take care of disbursement in Minsar in the morning. Tomorrow's market day; the jewelers and platemongers from Vellathil will be there, and they'll be glad to take the stuff off our hands. Tell the troops it'll be a straight percentage disbursement, and

I'm turning over my share to be divided up as a contribution to their funeral funds.'

Alla raised her eyebrows. 'You get hit on the head today, boss?'

'Nope, just want to make sure I'll have a volunteer force I can depend on in a few weeks. Meanwhile, broach a few barrels of that wine from our provident adversary's baggage train and distribute it among the troops. And let loose the dancing girls. Assuming they want to be loose.'

'Most of them are "loose" already.'

'Ouch. Just make sure they know they're free to go where they want.' Shel sighed. 'Anything else?'

Alla shook her head. 'All right,' Shel said. 'Telch?'

Telch put his head into the tent. 'Lord?'

'Lord' meant that Delmond was right outside. 'Bring in the prisoner,' said Shel.

A moment later, between two guards, Delmond swaggered into Shel's tent. They had taken away his trademark black armor, but even left only in hose and his quilted haqueton, he was still an imposing figure – broad-shouldered, muscular and stocky, his face presently twisted out of shape with anger. The only item of dress not usual for him was the iron collar locked around his neck, the infallible method for keeping a potential shapeshifter stuck firmly in the shape he was presently wearing.

Following him was a tall, fair, slender man dressed in a herald's tabard emblazoned with a large blue dog, seated toward the dexter. Both man and tabard were scrupulously clean, Shel noted, as the herald bustled forward to officiously dust off the remaining seat before the map table.

Delmond sat down with a grunt. The herald drew himself up and said, much more loudly than necessary, 'I proclaim to your graces the presence of my lord Delmond t'Lavirh of the Black Habiliment, prince of Elster and Lord Paramount of Chax—'

Both these titles were accurate enough, but neither was worth bragging that loudly about. Elster was so hereditarily subdivided a country that it had princes by the dozen, and Chax was a small but population-heavy area of Sarxos best known for its ironwood forests, its light red wines, its strategically important position at the confluence of two large rivers, and its habit of being passed from hand to hand of the major game-players about once every two weeks. Delmond, however, had come to rule Chax by accident . . . a fact which seriously amused some of Sarxos's more established and experienced players. Since he won it (by his adversary badly mismanaging a battle), he had been swanning around among the Kingdoms as if he were much more important than he really was. You got this kind of response with new players, sometimes – people who were lucky early on in their history. Occasionally they steadied down and became forces to be reckoned with. More often, they hit runs of bad luck in diplomacy or battle as spectacular as their good luck had been, got burned out, and left the game, or else they so seriously annoyed their fellow players that the most wildly assorted forces would sometimes be assembled for the express purpose of stamping out the 'new-sance,' publicly and with a flourish. So far Delmond hadn't yet achieved that status, but he was getting close.

Shel glanced at the herald, and then at Alla: and Alla said, not raising her voice, 'And here is Shel Look-behind of Talairn and Irdain, free leader of a free people, who today has beaten you in battle. We will now dictate terms.'

Azure Alaunt looked fastidiously shocked, as if someone had suggested a discussion about body odor. 'Hear now the words of the Lord Paramount of Chax—'

'He doesn't get to say anything,' Alla said, 'until the victor has spoken and named the terms under which he will accept your surrender.'

Azure Alaunt bristled. 'First my lord demands that you show proper courtesy to his army, the fiercely-armed, the mighty-thewed, we who have labored to tragic effect in the terrible toils of war today—'

'Excuse me,' Shel said to the herald. 'Were *you* in the battle today, Azure Alaunt? I don't think so, because you don't look at all like the rest of us, and you sure don't *smell* like the rest of us. So you can just lose the "we" part.'

'Ahem – remembering that none can stand alone against the massing forces of the Dark Lord. If we do not all hang together, we will all hang sep—'

'Oh, *please*, leave Ben Franklin out of this,' Shel said. 'As for the rest of it, well, "Dark Lord, shmark lord", that's what *I* say.'

Delmond's eyes widened: he opened his mouth, shut it again. 'Let's you and I get real now,' Shel said. 'You shouldn't find the attitude so odd, because you sold out *your* contract with the Dark Forces and went freelance as soon as you had a chance. A dim move, but you don't need me to tell you that now, though everyone did try to warn you earlier. Even your mother. And *now* here you sit hoping that out of the dumbness, I mean the goodness of my heart, I'll be merciful, and "respect the usages of war," and save your butt from the mess you've gotten it into.'

He took a longish drink of honeydraft. 'Well, I have news for you. The "usages of war" as they are honored in Sarxos means that I can dispose of an unransomed prisoner as I see fit. My wizards have been talking to all potentially interested parties since earlier this afternoon. They can't reach your mother, by the way; her under-wizards say this is "her day to wash her hair." There have been no offers of ransom for you . . . even when we discounted you: sorry. So unless there is an offer by tomorrow at this time, which frankly I doubt, *I* can do with you, personally, whatever I like.'

Shel sat back and contemplated his cup of honeydraft for a moment. Alla watched Delmond unwinkingly, smiling, like a cat waiting to see which way a rat will jump. 'Now, *I* for one think it would be just a ton of fun to see you dragged off into eternal servitude in the slave pits of Oron the Lord of the Long Death. See, here's the note he sent me this afternoon, requesting the pleasure of your company.' Shel reached across his map table and poked the smoking scrap of parchment with his knife, wishing privately that the ink on it would stop smoking. The effect was unsettling, and he kept worrying that the note would set fire to something valuable. 'Not a ransom offer: it's an offer to *buy* you. And there are about two hundred other generals, lords and ladies, and petty and grand nobility of the Great and Virtual Dominion of Sarxos who would strongly suggest that I take the offer. However, I don't like slavery much, and I'm persuaded by my quartermaster that it would be much better business to simply asset-strip you and turn you out to beg for your bread on the roads, so that the peasants whose lives you've made miserable by burning their fields and destroying their livelihoods can throw herdbeast patties at you as you pass.'

Delmond shivered visibly. 'Surely it would be more useful to you, politically speaking I mean, to impound my army and send me and my property home with a suitable escort—'

'Excuse me?' Shel stuck one finger in his ear and began digging. 'I could have sworn I heard you claim to have an army. That pitiful crowd of leftover wannabe skinheads in the corral out there, the bike-chained, the saggy-butted, those two hundred people with no horses and no weapons: *that* army? Oh.'

It had long been said of Delmond that he could not understand irony. Shel now found this to be true. 'Not this army,' Delmond said hurriedly. 'My other one.'

Shel laughed out loud. 'I'm sorry,' he said. 'If you do have another one stashed away somewhere, which I'm not sure I believe, they won't be yours for long. Not after word of this afternoon gets out.' And Shel very much hoped that this was true. It was likely enough that Delmond *could* have another army . . . but that was no admission which Shel was prepared to make today. 'And even if you have another, why would I want it, considering the quality of your troops? If "quality" is the word I'm looking for.'

'Land, then.'

Shel sighed. 'I don't want your lands.' *Much*, he thought, but this was no time to discuss his personal ambitions with Delmond. Today's battle was part of a long string of initiatives discussed with two other Sarxonian generals whom Shel trusted . . . well, trusted as far as you could trust *anyone* who was playing in Sarxos: about throwing distance, usually. If things went well, sometime in the next few months Shel would come in and take Delmond's lands by force, and everybody in Sarxos, including the people who lived there, would wholeheartedly approve the change. For the moment, though, Shel said, 'No thanks . . . I'm much more interested in your portable assets, and it serves you right to lose them. I can't imagine why you carry all this junk around with you, except that you're too spoiled to eat off normal dishes in the field, like everyone else. Half an acre of brocade for one tent, half a ton of gold plate, a dozen suits of ceremonial armor, a brigade of dancing girls . . .'

'You cannot take these from me! They are the royal regalia of my house from time immemorial—'

'Delmond, I've taken them *already*. You *lost* the fight today. This is the 'dictating terms' part of the battle:

haven't you noticed? And anyway, you stole nine-tenths of this stuff from Elansis of Schirholz a year and a half ago. Sacked her castle when only her little brother the Young Landgrave was home, with an insufficient force to defend it. Very nasty, Delmond, stealing the family silver from nine-year-olds . . . I guess it's no wonder you won't leave this stuff at home: you're afraid someone might try the same trick on *you*. Well, you've outsmarted yourself, because all this stuff now counts as "spoils of war," having been taken fair and square on the battlefield. If you'd left it home, no one would be able to touch it. But Elansis'll be really glad to get the Eye of Argon back again: it'll mean that something will grow in Schirholz's fields this year, and Talairn will acquire a couple of powerful allies which will raise eyebrows from here to the Sundown Sea. *That* will serve you right, too. I can't *believe* you stole that thing. It's common knowledge that the Crimson Emerald will bring ruin on anyone who handles it except members of the Landgraves' House. Don't tell me your mother put you up to that, *too*?'

Delmond acquired a stunned expression. Shel considered it a moment and filed it away under 'Mothers/stepmothers, wicked, extreme caution when dealing with.' 'Right,' Shel said. 'Meanwhile, your surviving nobles will be cared for and ransomed as per the usual procedure . . . fortunately, we have had a good number of offers for *them*. Your surviving infantry will spend a month at labor in Minsar, by way of reparation for the damage they've caused to Talairn territory, and they'll then be released. Who knows, some of them may want to stay with us afterwards. A poorly-fed-looking lot, they are. *You*, however, will have a meal tonight and a meal in the morning, and then we'll give you the statutory skin of water and bag of bread and meat, and a horseman will take you ten miles back into your borderlands so that you can start walking home. You might get there by midsummer, if you don't dawdle. The collar stays on, by the way. Flying back home in bird or bat shape wouldn't give you nearly enough time to reflect on the error of your ways.'

Delmond turned a wonderful color of puce, drew a long breath, and began saying dreadful things about Shel's background and parentage. He was just starting to hit his stride when a soft moaning noise began radiating from near the tentpole. Ululator was shivering slightly, just enough so that you could see the pattern-welding in the metal shift and move, as if the steel breathed, and the howling got louder. It was like the sound a tomcat makes when threatening another tom . . . except this was louder, and the threat was absolutely personal, like the angry note in your mother's voice when she works out why you've been in the bathroom with the door locked for so long.

Delmond abruptly gulped and went silent. 'I think you should moderate your language,' Shel said. 'Howler has been known to get out of my tent at night and go about her own business – I wouldn't go so far as to say her "lawful occasions". The things she does aren't strictly legal. But I always pay for the funerals afterwards.'

Delmond was now sitting very still.

'So that's the way it's going to be,' said Shel. 'Azure Alaunt, as a constituted herald of the Dominion, say you now: is the disposition within the law?'

'It is within the law,' said the herald, looking with slight nervousness at his employer.

'Fine. I will now hear any formal protest of the disposition.'

Delmond fought first for air, then for words, and after a moment, he burst out, 'None of this would have happened if you had not had magic on your side! It was not horses that bore you down the hillsides at us, but devils! We will find out where to get such demons of our own, and then we will crush you where you—'

'They come from Altharn, mostly,' said Shel mildly. 'A nice little stud farm up there: I own it. We cross-breed our black Delvairns with the mountain ponies, and there's rumored to be a secret ingredient in the mixture . . . possibly goat. Don't think you'll have much luck with them though, Delmond. They bite, and you just have to put up with it . . . because it's their spirit that makes them so surefooted.'

'Spirits,' cried Delmond, turning to Azure Alaunt, 'did you hear that, he *admits* it, they were spirits, familiars—'

Azure Alaunt glanced ever so briefly at Shel – an expression of utter hopelessness which his master did not see, and which made Shel wonder if, at some much later date, he should offer the man a job.

'Mmmm,' said Shel to Delmond. 'Not your usual level of response. Things must be getting tough down at the Wal-Mart.'

29

Delmond went rather darker than puce. It was not considered in the very best taste to refer inside Sarxos to a player's 'real life' outside. The game was supposed to be a relief from 'outside,' after all, a place where the players could leave the pressures and mundanity of their lives, and experience something bigger and more exotic in company with many others intent on the same thing. But then lots of things happened in Sarxos which were not strictly 'by the book,' a fact which the game's creator apparently took as an indicator that the game was progressing correctly, and was in fact becoming its own place, its own self . . . something slightly alive. And anyway, Delmond had bent a fair number of the rules himself in this engagement. Turnabout was fair play, Shel thought.

'All right,' Shel said. 'The disposition is made. Talch?' The guard reappeared. 'Take him out and feed him. Then lock him up in a baggage cart for the move up the road – not one of his, one of ours: who knows what little surprises he's got built into his own equipment. Have the regulation beggar's bag ready for him in the morning. And what the heck, why should we be stingy? . . . Throw a lump of hard cheese in it.'

Shivering with rage, but silent now, Delmond was taken out. Azure Alaunt paused on the threshold of the tent and said, 'A word in your ear, lord, if I may—'

Shel nodded.

'His mother is not a safe person to offend. If harm should come to her son on the road – your own play could be damaged.'

Shel sat quiet for a moment. 'Boldly spoken,' he said

then. 'And possibly even true. I take your warning at its face value, Azure Alaunt.'

The herald bowed and slipped out of the tent.

Shel sat still for a moment more, chewing his lip in a thoughtful way. 'A little twitchy, that lad,' said Alla, getting up and stretching.

'Maybe. Come on,' Shel said, getting up as well. 'Let's have the baggage people get this tent down, and get ourselves up the road to Minsar, and our dinners. We've done a good day's work.'

Alla nodded, went out of the tent.

A moment later, Shel went out into the near-darkness too, and walked off a short distance through the red sticky mud, trying to find a solid spot. Finally he found one, a place which by some magic had not been completely poached into mire by the thousands of hooves, and looked southward at the first moon, the smaller one, now floating low over the mist.

He turned to look north, toward Minsar, between the wooded hills. The upward-reaching tips of the pine trees were slightly paler than the rest of the branches in the moonlight: polished matte-silver as opposed to the slightly tarnished silver and shadow-black of the trees. It had just turned spring in the south continent, and by daylight you would correctly see the color at the tips of the conifers as that particular shade of young green. Elsewhere would be the thin faint veiling of green on the opening buds of the oaks and maples; everything shone fresh and new. The fields were dazzling in the mornings; besides the yellow of nevermind in the grass, and the white of the south-continent daisy that comes after the snow, there was other whiteness, too – the new lambs, bouncing around on unsteady legs in the spring sunshine, astounded and overjoyed to be alive. So when you got the news that somebody like Delmond was at your borders, about to cross over and stamp everything into a bloody pulp – the villages, the people, the lambs and the daisies, everything that mattered and many things that hadn't, until now – you got cranky, and you stood up to defend the place.

Shel had started doing that, much to his own surprise, some while back. Shel rarely saw daisies except at the florist's down the road, and had never seen a lamb that wasn't in plastic-wrapped pieces at the supermarket meat counter . . . but in Sarxos he had come to know what flowers, and livestock, meant to country people, to the small farmers and smallholders among whom he had moved. And when he had first 'settled' and made this part of Sarxos his home-away-from-home, and someone else in Sarxos had come along, intent on taking the livestock, and killing the people and the daisies – not even out of need, but out of what that person considered political expediency – Shel said, 'The hell with that,' and had started raking together an army.

That first battle now seemed a long time ago . . . that, and the problems that followed 'saving his country' for the first time. Armies, no matter how small – and his was – have a distressing tendency to want to be paid. If their pay is late, they tend to go elsewhere, or turn on you. Shel had found ways to pay them, out of his own pocket sometimes, thereby acquiring a reputation among other generals and rulers in Sarxos as an eccentric. Then along had come the original rulers of 'his country,' roused from long neglect of it by the action: rulers who felt (with some cause) that Talairn was *their* property, and who disliked someone raising an army to defend it without their permission. That particular disagreement had gone on for nearly a year, until the rulers realized that fighting with Shel was getting them nowhere, and that the price he was offering them, to buy them off, was actually pretty good. After that, by and large, he had been left alone . . . except by the likes of Delmond. When people like him turned up in Talairn, Shel stomped on them as best he could . . . because he had fallen in love with the place. He knew that was always dangerous: love, and that you were likely to be wounded.

. . . But some wounds were worth it.

Shel stood there for a few breaths more, looking out at the moonlight, and then said: 'Gameplay ends here.'

Everything around him suddenly acquired the perfectly frozen look of a still photograph or holo. 'Options,' said the voice of the server which controlled the 'frame' for the virtual experience. 'Continue: save: save and continue.'

'Save,' Shel said. 'Accounting, please.'

'Saved. Accounting for Shel Lookbehind,' said the master games computer, as the frozen backdrop began, slowly, to dissolve into process blue. 'Balance carried forward from previous gameplay: four thousand eight hundred and sixteen points. Score accrued in this session: five hundred and sixty points. Total balance: five thousand three hundred and seventy-six points. Query?'

'No query,' Shel said.

'Confirming accounting accepted, no query. Read waiting messages now?'

'Save for later,' said Shel.

'Acknowledged,' said the master games computer. 'Please enter your personal satchel codes for an archival save of this result.'

Shel blinked twice, summoning up his computer's copy of the satchel code 'signature' which infallibly verified the game's results as his own to the master games computer. The signature was complex, too much so for an opponent to fake: one part of the code changed with each session, and was combined with a second part which resided permanently in his machine, and a third which the 'master' Sarxos machine maintained. No save could be performed without all three, and no one could get at any character's profile, nor could the game be re-entered, without the combination of all three codes. Shel nodded to the computer, locking in his 'save'—

'Save confirmed,' said the computer. He blinked a little, realizing for the first time that its voice was really a lot like Alla's. 'This session of Sarxos^{SM} is completed. Sarxos is copyright ©Christopher Rodrigues, 1999, 2000, 2003-2010 and subsequent years. All rights reserved universe-wide and in all other universes which may be discovered.'

—And everything vanished. Once more Shel was sitting in a room crammed with books and tapes and all the other impedimenta of his life, and (taking up most of the room) with the big easy chair which let him line up his implant with the link in his home computer. There Shel sat, yawning, in the flesh rather than 'in the flash,' at six in the morning in his apartment in Cincinnati, with the dawn beginning to lever its way in through the blinds: and his flesh began to complain to him that after a long night of campaigning, it was stiff and sore. The machinery was supposed to speak to your muscles a few times an hour, to keep them contracting: but sometimes these routine movements just weren't enough to get rid of the excess lactic acid that built up in the big muscles when you were under stress. Because of this, steady long-term players were likely to do weights and get a lot of exercise on a regular basis: there might be a stereotype that suggested people who VR'd too much were thin and flabby, but Sarxos players tended toward a surprisingly high level of fitness. You could hardly campaign effectively enough to win a kingdom if your body wouldn't support your gameplay . . .

Meanwhile, his body was saying something very specific to him. *CORNFLAKES!* It shouted. *CORNFLAKES AND MILK!*

Shel got up and stretched, grinning at the thought of something to eat, and at the look on Delmond's face when he had realized he wasn't going to be cut loose with his assets intact for the sake of pleasing his mother. *Tarasp of the Hills*, Shel thought, looking for his housekeys: *what are we going to do about you, lady? You're a menace, even to your own flesh and blood. I've got to talk to the wizards about this . . .*

He changed into a less rumpled T-shirt, locked his apartment and went down the stairs two at a time to the street, in extremely cheerful mood. Despite it being a Saturday, he wouldn't be free today. Evening shift at the hospital started at three-thirty: it would be yet another exciting evening of drawing bloods and collecting labwork samples on about a hundred patients, every one of whom loathed the sight of him. Yet despite all this, as he swung into the convenience store and got his cornflakes and his milk, and spent ten minutes or so shooting the breeze with Ya Chen, the night lady, before she went off shift, Shel's heart sang. *What a terrific campaign. What a terrific battle. I can't wait to start dealing with the can of worms that this will have cracked open . . .*

All the way back from the 7-11 he was laying plans . . . thinking about which players he needed to consult. The continuing threat from the Dark Lord was on his mind: exactly what *had* he meant by that offer to 'buy' Delmond? The amount offered had been three times Delmond's potential ransom value. Unless it was some clandestine arrangement of Delmond's mother's with the Dark One. *I wouldn't put it past her*, Shel thought as he went up the stairs at a run. *She's a snake, that one. In fact*, wasn't *she a snake originally? Some kind of—*

He stopped at his apartment's landing, with his keys in his hand, and stared at the door. It was ajar.

Don't tell me I left this open.

He pushed the door open, cautiously, and peered in.

His heart seized. Someone had been in here. Someone had been in . . .

. . . and had trashed the place.

He walked softly through, half-wondering whether the intruder might still be there – and half not caring: because at the far side of the living room, where his desk was, and his chair with his interface . . . was a disaster area. The desk was overturned. The computer lay on its side, its main system box pulled open, the boards everywhere. His monitor was smashed. His system was destroyed.

Naturally Shel got right on the phone and called the insurance company. Naturally, eventually, they'd pay for a new system. But the one thing they could do nothing about was his hard drive. Shel would find, later, when he got the hard disk to the shop on Monday, that it had been formatted, and then his last hopes died.

He had not backed up his files to his 'emergency' storage before he left. Most particularly, he had not backed up his satchel codes, the complex and completely unrememberable codes which, combined with the codes saved in the master Sarxos games server, gave him access to his character and his character's history. It would take weeks to get this mess ironed out. Sarxos people were obsessively careful about their security. Oh, he'd get back eventually. He'd submit the results of his last save from his remote backups — like many users these days he subscribed to a 'lifesaver' service, an offsite secondary storage for backups — and copies of the satchel codes used in that save. But by then, this years' campaigning would be over. Two years' careful preparation of the ground for this year's campaigning, two year's amiable scheming with other players – all shot to hell. Some of the people Shel had been conspiring with would be furious. They'd want nothing to do with him in the future, regardless of the fact that what had happened to him was not his fault. Others, missing him, might simply move on to other alliances.

And what about Alla? If she was real, she might just drift away for lack of the player she'd been working with. And if she *wasn't* real, she might just be erased. That happened when game-generated characters weren't interacted with on a regular basis. The possibility that Alla might cease to exist because of his absence, bothered him intensely.

He started again, of course. It was not in Shel's nature to give up easily: that was one of the things that had made him stand out as a Sarxos player to start with. But as he slowly began the business of rebuilding this part of his life which had meant so much to him, his heart still bled for what he'd lost . . . and the question remained unanswered:

Why?

Some days later, it was seven-thirty in the morning, and Megan O'Malley was in the kitchen, rummaging in the cupboards and muttering to herself. 'I can't believe we're out of it *again* . . .'

Having four older brothers had posed many problems over the course of the years, but the worst was that none of them ever stopped eating: or at least that was the way it looked. You would come in for your breakfast, ready to stuff something hurriedly into your face before heading out to school, and find that the kitchen had been stripped bare like some third-world cropland after the locusts had passed through. When the brothers got old enough to go away to college, those of them that did, Megan had hoped the situation might improve: but instead, it only got worse – Mike and Sean had seemed to start eating *more* to compensate for Paul's and Rory's absence. Hiding food from the two who were studying close to home at GWU and Georgetown worked only occasionally – usually, if the food was something they didn't want – and there were unfortunately too few kinds of food that fell into that category. Muesli had been one, for a while . . . until late one night Sean, while rifling the cupboards, had stumbled across Megan's supply. She had had to start moving the stuff around, after that. Sometimes this tactic worked.

Not always. 'Locusts,' Megan muttered in disgust as she picked up the box she had thought safely hidden down under the sink, behind the bleach and the rubber gloves. It was a box of the genuine Swiss muesli, Familia, not one of the sawdust-tasting local brands. It was an *empty* box.

She stood up in the big sunny golden-tiled kitchen and sighed, then chucked the Familia box in the trashcan and headed for the counter where the bread-box lived, and opened it.

No bread. *So much for toast,* Megan thought, letting the breadbox lid fall. *It's a pity I don't need to lose any weight, because I'd be starting. Oh well. Tea . . .*

That, at least, she found: her brothers, mercifully, had all become coffee drinkers as soon as it became plain to her parents that it would not stunt their growth (and that, in cold fact, probably nothing could.) Megan put water in the kettle, put it on the stove, turned the 'hot' burner up to full, and went off to find a mug, glancing at the clock. *Seven-forty-five. Half an hour before my ride shows up . . . might as well check the mail.*

She headed into the downstairs den, a big room which housed one of the family's three networked computers, and which was otherwise stuffed full, from floor to ceiling and around all four walls, with her father's and mother's research books. When your mom was a reporter for the *Washington Post,* and your dad was a mystery writer, this made for a fairly eclectic and occasionally haphazard-seeming collection, and every-thing inevitably got mixed together, so that books on international politics and economics and the environ-ment and world history, and slightly weird volumes like *Nameless Horrors and What To Do About Them* and *Luftwaffe Secret Projects 1946,* wound up shelved with or piled on top of a truly terrifying collection of books on forensics and weapons and poisons, books with titles like *Snobbery with Violence* and *The Do's and Don'ts of Committing the Perfect Crime* and *The A-Z of Venomous*

Animals and Glaister's *Medical Jurisprudence and Toxicology*. Megan knew her father was perfectly law-abiding and utterly gentle – she had once seen him weep when he'd accidentally killed a mouse he was trying to catch and release outside, after one of the cats had turned it loose in the house – but all the same she hoped fervently that no one would ever suspect him of a murder: once they got a look at the downstairs den, no human being could possibly believe that he wouldn't have known exactly how to do it.

She sat down in the computer chair and sighed at the sight of the inevitable pile of books on the table in front of the main interface box. No matter how many times she reminded them, her father and mother kept leaving their current research material obstructing the working pathway between the machine and the implant chair ... but then they used retinal/optical implants, which lined up with the machine well above the level of the table, and Megan's was one of the newer type of implant, a side-looking neck-neural or 'droud', which lined up from a lower angle. As Megan pushed this morning's heap of books aside – her dad's, mostly: he typically stayed up writing until three or four in the morning – she looked them over with mild interest. The pile included, at its top, copies of *Thomas Cook European Railway Timetable*, *Jane's Guns Recognition Guide*, and *The Curry Club Book of 250 Hot And Spicy Dishes*. She blinked at that one: the potential 'plot' for what he was working on had been shaping itself up perfectly until then. *Lure someone onto an obscure eastern European train, shoot them – and then put them in a curry . . .?*

. . . Naah. All the same, she resolved to stop at the store on the way home and pick up some yogurt. If Dad was thinking about making dinner tonight, it would be good for putting out the fire when the chillies got too incendiary.

Megan swiveled the computer chair around into the right position: it took a moment to 'remember' her favorite settings, raised her feet up a little, tilted back at the right angle. Megan lined up her implant with the computer's master interface box, and felt the familiar tiny shock of interconnection, like someone throwing a light switch down in your bones: switching the normal universe off, and another one *on*—

Megan knew that some people organized their personal virtual 'workspaces' as just one more office full of file cabinets. She scorned such smallness of mind. When anything was possible in virtual reality, why didn't people do, well, *anything*? For the way they behaved, she had no answers. For herself, she now walked out into the middle of a gigantic stone amphitheater, the tiers and tiers of worn white limestone seating reaching up a couple of stories above her. Above the top tier of seats, black sky with fierce white stars burning in it reached up to the zenith. She looked over her shoulder, out past the 'front' of the amphitheater, to see a long 'downward' slope of dimly lit pink-stained ice and grit, dusted with bluish methane snow; and low above the horizon, hanging there fat and oblate and orange as an overripe peach, Saturn hovered, his rings rakishly tilted to one side, the long shadow from the sunward side striping the planet's surface at a slewed and stylish diagonal. Light reflecting up from the planet's surface dusted the surface of the moon Rhea with a pale golden bloom. Like the Moon, Rhea never turned this face away from her primary: but Megan knew that if she stood there long enough watching, Saturn would slowly start to wane, the rings would shift, and soon the sun would come up over Rhea's too-close little horizon and change the predominant color of the moon from soft gold to blazing ice-white, with a great shadow thrown over the amphitheater from the high edge of the nearby impact basin Tirawa.

Unfortunately Megan had a lot of other things to do this morning besides planet watch. 'Chair,' she said, and one provided itself behind her, a close duplicate of the one at home. She sat back and put her feet up, and said to the computer, 'Mail, please?'

'Running mail,' said the computer, in a pleasant female voice, and started displaying a set of frozen, caption-tagged video-audio 'thumbnails' of her waiting messages, without any fuss. Other people might want to personify their computer as a 'secretary' which would talk to them in the shape of a person, offer to show them their correspondence, and so on, but Megan preferred to have a machine which simply did the work she told it to, *when* she told it. She didn't care for chatty interfaces with overbearing personalities. ('That's because you've already got one of your own,' Mike had said to her when she had mentioned this to him, some months back. Mike had complained about the ensuing bruises for some days thereafter. *Served him right*, Megan thought, smiling slightly at the memory. *If he can't take the trouble to learn enough martial arts to keep his little sister from laying him out flat occasionally, well, it's hardly my problem . . .*

The mail was mostly nothing important. 'First one,' Megan said, and that small thumbnail picture suddenly swelled to full size and three dimensions and began speaking to her. The label underneath it identified it as having come from her high school guidance counselor. Mr MacIlwain was sitting behind his desk, which rather resembled her parents', covered with papers and disks and books and heaven knew what else. 'This is a reminder that your runthrough for the SAT III and SAT IV/NMSQT tests has been rescheduled for March 12th. If you've requested Advanced Placement Examinations as well, this runthrough has been rescheduled for March 15th. The English Composition with Essay examination will be given nationally only in April, so make sure that you—'

'Yeah, yeah, stop, erase,' Megan said. She had taken care of everything mentioned in the message, and was as ready for her SAT's as she was ever going to be – though every time she looked at the Advanced Placements date, she thought, *The Ides of March, oh, great . . .* As if Shakespeare and Julius Caesar hadn't done enough to curse that date. Still, the real exam itself was a month and more away from that. *Another month to spend twitching . . .* 'Next,' she said.

The next thumbnail blew itself up into the shape of

Carrie Henderson, another junior at her high school. 'Megan, hi! Look, I know you said you weren't really interested in the dance committee, but we could really really *really* use a—'

'Stop,' Megan said, 'save.' *I really really* really *don't want to be involved in this. Let someone else do it. If I just ignore this for a while, she'll probably find someone else to do it anyway* . . . 'Next—'

The third thumbnail blew itself up into a man in a suit and tie holding up a sample of carpet, and standing on a seemingly unending acreage of the stuff, in a horrendous paisley pattern which ran up against the edge of Megan's amphitheater and mercifully vanished there. 'Dear systems user,' the man said excitedly, 'your address has been especially chosen as that of one of an elite group of users who will be able to appreciate the value of—'

'Stop, erase!' Megan moaned. *Cyberspam . . . there must be* some *way to stop it . . .* She found herself wondering whether any of the anti-cyberspam initiatives which Net Force was presently backing were *ever* going to make it successfully through Congress. The problem was that the 'spam' lobbies were so powerful . . . and as soon as the government found a way to stop one kind, another sprang up. It meant that her mailbox, as well as nearly everybody else's she knew, kept getting cluttered with ads she didn't want. At least the carpet ad had been fairly innocuous. Some of the ads that wound up in her mailbox were so annoying or insistent that she wanted to start practicing thrust-kicks on the computer, or better still, the people who sent the ads . . .

The water must almost be boiling, she thought, glancing at the remaining few thumbnail captions. *There's nothing really important here, these can wait—*

An abrupt soft chime sounded in the air all around her, and Megan looked about her in surprise: someone was trying to reach her for live chat. *At this hour?* 'Who is it?' she said to the computer.

'Message ID shows James Winters,' the computer said.

'Really? Wow,' Megan said. 'Accept—'

Off to one side of the amphitheater there suddenly appeared an office somewhat tidier than her father's and mother's. Early morning sun was streaming through the Venetian blinds in its windows, and lay in broad stripes on the big desk in the foreground of the office. Behind the desk, which was empty at the moment except for a few printouts and letters and a few stacked disks, sat the big broad-shouldered form of James Winters, Net Force's public relations liaison, and the senior contact for the Net Force Explorers. He pushed aside the piece of paper he had been glancing at, and gazed 'out' at Megan, looking for the moment, in his suit, very much like some harried businessman, except for the Marine haircut and the lazy eyes. Those eyes might be all netted with smile lines, but there was a toughness in them that most businessmen could only wish to achieve.

'Megan? I hope I haven't caught you at a bad time.'

'No, I was getting ready to go to class, but that's not for a few minutes yet.' *But you would have known that,* she thought, getting interested: Winters was intimately knowledgeable about all the Net Force Explorers' schedules. *Something's up!*

He nodded, looking past her briefly. 'Hey, nice view.'

Megan smiled slightly. 'Yeah, it's summer "here". For about the next six hours, anyway, if you can really call it a summer when the axis tilts by only a third of a degree. How can I help you?'

He looked at her thoughtfully. 'Megan, just check me on something. Your profile shows you as being a Sarxos player.'

Her eyebrows went up. 'I drop in there every now and then.'

'More than every couple of weeks, say?'

She thought. 'Yeah, I'd say so. Maybe once a week on the average, though sometimes more often if something exciting starts happening. But it's a good place to just wander around in, even when there's not a war or a feud between wizards going on. Interesting people there . . . and Rodrigues did a good job on the game. It "feels" realer than a lot of virtual games do.'

He nodded. 'What have you heard about players being "bounced"?'

Megan blinked at that. 'You mean, people's satchel codes being wiped out? Viruses and that kind of thing? I've heard that it does happen, sometimes. Revenge, supposedly. Someone taking things too seriously . . .'

'Someone, if it's just someone, is taking things a lot too seriously lately. There have been something like twelve people bounced in the last year.'

That came as news to Megan. 'One a month . . . but

there are hundreds of thousands of players in Sarxos. It doesn't seem like much.'

'It wouldn't to me either, unless I knew there hadn't been *any* bounces for the eight years ending a year and a half ago. Something's going on, and the companies which sponsor Sarxos are getting twitchy. They would hate to have to shut the server down—'

'I just bet,' Megan said, somewhat dryly. Sarxos players paid by the session or in a yearly 'subscription' flat fee. Either way, there would be a lot of money involved, potentially millions and millions of dollars over any given year.

'Well, we just had a particularly emphatic bounce,' Winters said. 'I'm not going to identify the player by real name, obviously, but a fellow who went by the character-name Shel Lookbehind—'

'Jeez, *Shel?*' Megan said, astonished.

'Did you know him?'

'A little, yeah,' Megan said. 'I ran across him while he was campaigning about a year ago. A lot of people got interested in those skirmishes he was having with the Queens of the Mordiri. There weren't any protocols for one person taking over another's territory before it had officially been declared abandoned, and everyone else wanted to see if any precedents were going to be set. I went down to Talairn to see what was going on there. Shel seemed like a good player, like a really nice guy. At least, his character did.'

'Well, the character is in limbo now, as you might expect,' said Winters. 'And this has been the most physically violent of the bounces so far, which is why it came to our attention. Most of them, as you said, have been caused by "a person or persons unknown" infecting the victim's system with a Trojan or virus of one kind or another. Additionally, there was at least one theft of a home system which may or may not have been a bounce. The evidence isn't conclusive. But in Shel's case, somebody broke into his apartment, wrecked the place, wiped his primary storage, and pretty much destroyed his system.'

Megan shook her head. 'And nobody has any idea of who it was?'

'Nothing that the local police department's forensics have been able to turn up, anyway. But I was hoping that you might be able to help out a little.'

'You want me to go into Sarxos and 'ask a few questions'?' Megan said.

'You'd be good for the job. You have a pre-established identity – which is handy: any new character who came in and suddenly started asking about the bounces would attract attention and suspicion immediately. But not just you. I think it would be smart, under the circumstances, to have someone working with you. Another viewpoint could be helpful . . . and Sarxos is, after all, a very big place. There's a lot of ground to cover.'

Megan chewed her lip thoughtfully. 'Someone else in the Net Force Explorers?'

'Preferably.'

She thought about that for a few moments. 'I have to confess I'm not sure which of the Net Force Explorers I know might be "players". You don't usually ask.'

'Well,' Winters said, 'I know of at least one other Explorer with an established identity who's expressed an interest, and doesn't mind if other Explorers know he's playing. Do you know Leif Anderson?'

Megan was caught by surprise one more time. 'You mean the Leif Anderson who lives in New York? The redheaded guy with all the languages? *He's* in Sarxos?'

'Yes. He plays a—' Winters stopped and looked down at the paper he was holding, and chuckled. 'A "hedge-wizard," it says here. I'm assuming that isn't someone who works on your garden using magic.'

Megan snickered. 'No. It's a classification that means you're concentrating on doing small wizardries instead of the big dangerous ones. It can either mean that you prefer to work close to the land and the "common people," or that you're not very good at what you do and you're trying to cover yourself. Hedge-wizards are supposed to be a little on the incompetent side.'

Winters looked bemused. 'Right. Well, will it be a good cover, do you think?'

'It should be,' Megan said, considering it. 'Hedge-wizards are always traveling around looking for rare herbs and weird spells and deeds to do. They usually get to know a lot of people. My character does the same kind of thing, but for different reasons . . . so it should work.'

'Should I have him get in touch with you, then?'

'Sure,' Megan said. 'Can it wait until tonight? Life around here is a little busy today.'

'No problem. Take this at your own pace. I would much rather you two took your time; rushing in and digging around too earnestly is likely to make the person or persons responsible go quiet . . . and you don't want that.'

'Nope. I'll need a list of the other characters who've been bounced,' Megan said.

'Right here,' said Winters. With another soft chime, a small slowly rotating pyramid, the symbol for a file waiting to be opened, appeared in Megan's workspace, hovering in the air near her. 'If you have any other questions, or if there's anything else you need, get in touch.'

'Right, Mr Winters. Thanks!'

He and his office vanished. Megan sat there, beginning to feel much more excited than was good for her with what now looked like an interminably long school day still to come. It was one thing to know you were a Net Force Explorer, affiliated (however loosely) to people doing work that could be about the most exciting there was. It was something else entirely to actually be on an assignment, with the people that you hoped you might someday work with watching you . . . interested and confident enough in your performance to give you a job and see what you did with it.

This, Megan thought, *is gonna be a blast*!

She got up out of the chair and told the computer, 'Break interface—'

—and found herself sitting in the chair in the den, with an unearthly shriek echoing around her. It came from the kitchen. Her mother's favourite kettle, the one with the train whistle in its spout, was now banging and clattering and whistling as if it was about to explode: and Megan's ride was outside, honking her horn.

Megan tore out into the kitchen to get the kettle off the stove before it burned its bottom out. *No tea . . .* she thought: but as she turned the stove off, and grabbed her computer pad and books and disks and house keycards off the kitchen table and dashed for the door, she was grinning with sheer exaltation.

Sarxos, here I come!

Chapter 2

Virtual Dominion of Sarxos:
Greenmonth 23, Year of the Dragon-In-The Rain

The tavern had only one room, and its roof was leaking. The rain which was falling softly and steadily outside was coming in through a bare place in the thatch, dripping morosely on the cracked slate hearth of the fireplace, and hissing and steaming where it hit. Smoke from the badly vented fireplace was rolling around, blue as smog, underneath the blackened rafters. A few sputtering lamps hung from those rafters, their light swimming in the smoke, some of the light actually making its way down to the ancient, massive, knife-scarred wooden tables underneath. At those tables sat a motley assortment of people, eating and drinking: peasant farmers in from the fields, nobles ostentatiously sitting on their folded-up cloaks so that they wouldn't have to physically touch the benches, mercenary soldiers in scarred leather armor, well-dressed foreign merchants talking animatedly among themselves about the Sarxonian investment markets and how the present wars would affect them: in other words, the usual Moons-day night crowd at the Pheasant and Firkin, everyone swilling down herbdraft or *gahfeh* or the host's watered (but fortunately unleaded) wine, eyeing one another suspiciously and having a good time. In the chimney-corner there was even the obligatory dark, hooded stranger with his feet up on one massive firedog, smoking a long pipe, his eyes glittering from under the hood as he watched the company. A large dingy-white cat with ragged ears and one eye gone milky-blind walked past the stranger, glanced at him, said, 'Huh. *You* again . . .' and kept on walking.

Leif Anderson, sitting at the far side of the tavern, alone at a small table near the door, looked around the tavern and thought absently that, in a way, it was the kind of place his mother had always warned him about. The problem was that, in her more protective moods, she was worried that he might stumble into a place like this in the real world, and he very much doubted that there *were* any: at least, not where he was likely to run into them, in New York or D.C. Outer Mongolia, possibly, or the Outer Hebrides, or the Yukon maybe. He smiled slightly. It always amused him when someone as tough as his mother, who had danced for years for the New York City Ballet, and therefore had a physique like spring steel and a tongue like a razor, got all worried about her 'little boy' – as if he had not inherited any of that toughness himself.

The innkeeper loomed over him suddenly. 'You using that other chair?' he said. He was an archetype, just as much as the guy by the fireplace: fat, balding, wearing an apron which had apparently last been washed before the present Dragon cycle began, and in perpetually foul temper.

Leif looked up. 'I'm waiting for someone,' he said.

'Great,' the innkeeper said, grabbing the spare chair with one hand. 'When he turns up, you can have another chair. I need this for the *paying* customers.'

Leif picked up the tankard of herbdraft he had been nursing and waved it meaningfully at the innkeeper.

'Tough,' the innkeeper said. 'You want another chair, you pay for another drink.' He started to laugh at his own alleged wit, exhibiting teeth like something from a dentist's horror novel.

'It is unwise,' Leif said, 'to insult a wizard.'

The innkeeper looked him over with a sneer, plainly unimpressed by what he saw – a slender young man in a somewhat ragged robe decorated with faded and obscure alchemical and magical symbols. 'You're nothing but a hedgie,' the innkeeper guffawed. 'What're you going to do? Not leave a tip?'

'No,' Leif said mildly, 'I'll give you a tip.' He pulled off his hat, fumbled around in it for a moment, and then came up with what he had been looking for. He threw it at the innkeeper, and said one word under his breath.

The innkeeper caught it by reflex – stared, for a moment, at what looked like a piece of rag tied up with string – and then got a startled expression. From nowhere, a puff of smoke appeared and wrapped itself around him. All around the inn, heads turned.

55

The smoke slowly cleared. Where the innkeeper had been standing, there was now a small white mouse sitting on the floor, looking around it in shock.

Leif leaned down and picked up the wrapped-up talisman from beside it. 'Even hedge-wizards,' he said, 'know some spells. That a good enough tip?' And he glanced under the next table before looking back at the mouse. 'Have a nice day.'

The mouse turned to see what had caught Leif's attention . . . and saw the beat-up white cat walking toward him with an expression that suggested it was ready for a pre-dinner snack.

The mouse ran off across the cracked and worn flagstones of the floor, with the cat heading after it, not really hurrying, just enjoying the prospect of its *hors-d'oeuvre*.

The other patrons of the inn turned away, not too concerned about this, since the innkeeper's daughter, totally unconcerned, began making the rounds and taking drink orders. Leif tucked his talisman away and sat back with his drink again, his attention distracted once more by the sound of the foreign merchants discussing the futures markets. Here, as in the real world, there was a hot trade among the merchants in hog-belly futures, and Leif had no trouble imagining his father sitting right here with these guys and talking margins and short-sells until the cows, or the hogs, came home. *I really should try to get him in here sometime*, Leif thought idly: *we might be able to make some 'money.'* His father's talent with investments, though, kept him hopping all over the planet, physically as well as virtually: so much so that he pretty much refused to spend his scarce leisure time anywhere virtual, or doing anything that sounded even slightly like 'talking shop.' *If I could get him in here, he'd probably much rather be some kind of berserk warrior in a loincloth. Anything to get out of a suit . . .*

Leif's attention was momentarily attracted by another of the patrons across the room, a tall, lean, intent young man in a dark jerkin who was methodically checking and cleaning a gun, some kind of semiautomatic with a Glock in its ancestry. Normally one might have expected this to cause some stir, but the Pheasant and Firkin was located in the little princedom of Elendra, and Elendra was one of the places in Sarxos where gunpowder didn't work. It didn't work in *most* places in Sarxos, actually. The creator of the game had been making his alternative world mostly for those who preferred strictly mechanical weapons, preferably the kind which meant you and your enemy had to get up close and personal to kill one another. But Chris Rodrigues had also apparently suspected that there would always be those for whom life would not be complete without weapons that went *BANG*, the more frequently and the more loudly the better, and for them, Sarxos had the adjacent countries of Arstan and Lidios, where explosives and other chemical-based weaponry were enabled. They were noisy places, featuring frequent wars with high body counts. Many Sarxonians made it a point to avoid Arstan and Lidios entirely, reasoning that it was better to let the boys and girls who were that way inclined just get on with what made them happy, and not distract or upset them with annoying visions of a world where people did business differently.

Apparently these visions *did* bother some players a little, for there were frequent attempts to find some explosive or gunpowder-analog which would work in the rest of Sarxos as well, despite the game-creator's insistence that there was no such substance, nor would there be. Some players – attempted alchemists, or would-be weapons dealers – would occasionally spend prolonged periods trying to invent such a substance. They tended to have accidents which were hard to explain except by the old Sarxonian saying: 'The Rules take care of themselves . . .'

The black cast-iron handle of the door near Leif turned: the door creaked open, swinging toward him and hiding his view. The patrons stopped what they were doing and stared – they would always do that, even if the person coming in was someone they knew. But it plainly wasn't, this time: they kept on staring.

The person who had come in now turned and shut the door. Medium height, slim build, long brown hair tied back tight and braided up around her head: dark clothes, all somber colors – brown tunic, black breeches and boots, a tight dark brown leather jerkin over it all, dark brown leather bands cross-binding the breeches: a dark brown robe over it all, divided up the back for riding, and a brown leather pack. If she was armed, Leif couldn't see where . . . not that *that* meant anything.

She looked around long enough to complete her part of the staring game – for it *was* a game: you had to meet the crowd's eyes, let them know you had as much right to be here as they did . . . otherwise there would be trouble, trouble that you might or might not start, but would definitely finish. The patrons of the Pheasant and Firkin, perceiving this, became elaborately uninterested in the new arrival.

She looked over at Leif. He lifted his hat again, enough to let her see the red hair.

She smiled and came over, sat down in the other chair, and looked around her with a wry expression.

'You come here often?' she said.

Leif rolled his eyes at the tired old line.

'No, I mean it seriously. This place is an utter dive: how'd you find it?'

Leif chuckled. 'I stumbled in last year, during the wars. It has a certain rural charm, don't you think?'

'It has *mice*,' Megan said, pulling her feet back a little and looking under the table at something that ran by. 'Oh, well, it doesn't matter, here comes the cat . . .'

Leif chuckled. 'You want something to drink? The tea's not bad.'

'In a while. I take it you got the list from Winters.'

'Yup . . . a few days ago.' Leif pushed the tea-tankard away from him and sat looking thoughtful. 'Parts of it surprised me. Problem is, if I knew those people at all, I knew most of them by their game-names and not by real-world names – otherwise maybe I would have caught on sooner. Probably a lot of people would have. But what's plain right away is that

59

all the people bounced were very active players. No dillies—' Leif used the Sarxos term for 'dilettantes,' people who played the Game less often than once a week. 'And as far as I can tell, no "minor" characters. All the people who got bounced were movers and shakers of one kind or another.'

Megan nodded: she apparently had noticed this, too. But she looked at him a little cockeyed. ' "A few days ago?" I would have thought you'd want to get started looking around here right away.'

'Oh, I did.' Leif grinned at her. 'But I wanted to do the first few pieces of groundwork on my own. If it turned out to be a waste of time, well, it was my time, not both of ours.'

'Oh. Okay. So where'd you go for your groundwork?'

'Up north, mostly.' Sarxos had two main continents, one north, one south. From the northerly one a great archipelago reached down in 'the Crescent' toward the southern, making thousands of suitable havens for pirates, rebels, and those who wanted to take a few weeks off from the business of gaming to work on their virtual tans. 'I was talking with a few people,' Leif said. 'One of them was a guy whose game-name was Lindau.'

' "Lindau" as in the storming of the Inner Harbor?' said Megan.

'Yup. Not that he's been storming much of anything since he was bounced. Also I had a chat with Erengis, who was Lindau's arch-enemy for so long. She's a regular gossip shop on two legs.' Leif stretched, glancing under the nearby table. 'And I talked to a few other people who were enemies of Shel's, or some of the other bounced people; and some of their friends.'

He must have looked a little smug, to judge by the expression on Megan's face. 'Right,' she said. 'And did one particular name come up at all? Several times, in fact?'

Leif smiled slightly. 'You're there before me.'

'Argath,' said Megan.

Leif nodded.

Argath was the king of Orxen, one of the more northerly countries, a place mountainous and short on resources, except for large numbers of barbarians clad in beastskins – people who loved to go to war at a moment's notice. The place had earned itself the cognomen 'The Black Kingdom' because of a tendency over many game-years to side with the Dark Lord during his periodic risings: yet somehow it never itself got overrun, a cause of considerable annoyance and envy to some other players.

Argath had insinuated himself into the kingship of Orxen over the last game-decade by means which were considered normal in Sarxos: he had made a name for himself as an effective general of the Orxenian forces during the period of rule of a weak and ineffective king. No one was terribly surprised when elderly King Laurin apparently had an accident near his fishpond late one night, and was found in the morning head down among the bemused koi by his body-servants, several hours drowned. No one was surprised when the murder failed to be pinned on anyone specific, and no one was surprised when Argath was elected king by acclamation, the unfortunate King Laurin having out-lived all his heirs.

Argath's career after that had been unremarkable, by Sarxonian standards. He campaigned in the summer, like most people did, and intrigued during the winter, setting up agreements with other players, or weaseling out of them. He won battles, and lost them, but mostly he won: Argath was good at what he did. Shel had fought him, a game-year or so previously, in the same kind of skirmish that Shel had had with Delmond: and Shel had won, which had surprised some of the locals – Argath's army had been much bigger than Shel's.

'And Argath,' Megan said, 'is not a construct – not an artifact or built-in feature of the game.'

'No, he's "live," I know,' Leif said. 'Someone told me once what he does in real life. It sure looks kind of like Argath might have it in for anybody who had beat him in a fair fight.'

'But only recently,' Megan said. 'All these bounces are within the last three years of game-time. Why would he just start going after people all of a sudden?'

'Why *wouldn't* he?' Leif shrugged. 'Something happens at home. Something snaps. All of a sudden he starts playing rough . . .'

'Well, maybe, but we don't have any evidence to support that idea,' Megan said, 'and Sherlock Holmes says it's a bad move to hypothesize without enough data. Anyway, all we've got so far is circumstantial evidence.'

'We've gotta start somewhere, though,' Leif said.

'Argath'll do, unless you can think of somewhere better.'

'I don't know if it's better,' Megan said. 'I had been thinking of going up to Minsar.'

'Where the last bounce happened.'

'Not so much because of the location itself. But that's where, as they say, "the eagles are gathered together." An army, even a little one, doesn't have its commander go missing-and-presumed-bounced without attracting a lot of attention: and that's where they'll be based until the situation sorts itself out . . . until they find a new lord to swear allegiance to, or decide to disband. We could find out a lot while everyone's descending on the place to do the sorting.'

'Sounds like a good bet. But I still think we should look into Argath.'

Megan made an 'oh-why-not' face. 'So exactly where *is* the big A at the moment?'

'Take a guess.'

'Minsar?' Megan looked bemused. 'You're kidding. What would he be doing *there*? Minsar's much too downmarket for him. One free city isn't going to keep his interest. Argath campaigns for whole countries. Look what he did over in Sarvent, and up north in Proveis! The city isn't at a spot of any great strategic value, either. The river's not even navigable up this far.'

'No one's really sure what he's doing there,' Leif said. 'Maybe the motive's just revenge. After all, Shel did beat him once. There's a power vacuum. Maybe now he thinks he can move in and take over.'

'I don't know.' She shook her head. 'Argath's been a

pretty subtle operator in the past. Why would he do something so obvious?'

'Carelessness,' Leif said. 'Certainty that he wouldn't get caught.'

'Well . . . maybe. But, look, it's like you say, we have to start somewhere . . .' Megan looked around. 'Who do we order a drink from in here?'

'The innkeeper's daughter. Her dad's busy.'

Maybe it was Leif's slight smile that made Megan give him a brief sharp look. Leif sat there looking innocent until the innkeeper's daughter came by. Megan ordered tea. When it came, she spent a few moments sipping it and looking thoughtful, while Leif turned his attention to watching something that was going on in the darkness under a table off to their right. 'So,' she said. 'How'll we get there? Walk? Or have you got horses outside?'

'Huh?' Leif looked up, briefly shocked. 'Uh, no. I fall off horses.'

'Oh.'

'Don't tell me. You ride.'

Megan made a wry face. 'Actually, it's not what I'm best at. I wouldn't mind just long-marching it, except that Minsar's some way from here, and I hate wasting the time.'

'Lucky for you you're traveling with a wizard, then,' Leif said. 'I have about three thousand miles saved up.'

He appreciated the quick relieved grin Megan flashed him. If you didn't have a horse to help you get around Sarxos, or some other means of transport, like a litter-bearing team, or a tame basilisk to ride, you usually wound up walking . . . and it could seem to take forever: part of the designer's plan to have you 'really experience' his world. But players who chose to could take the points they accrued in play, not as money or power, but as transit: the ability to (with the use of the proper rapid-transit spell, one so simple even nonwizards could manage it) simply disappear from one spot and appear in another. Armies could not use this facility: Rodrigues had been quoted as saying that that would be 'too damn much like real life.' But people traveling peaceably in company could use it to go wherever they liked.

'That's a lot of miles,' Megan said. 'What have you been *doing* in here to earn all that?'

'The usual hedge-wizard stuff,' Leif said. 'Healing the sick . . . raising the dead.'

Megan raised an eyebrow. Few wizards in Sarxos were quite *that* powerful. 'Well, healing the sick, anyway,' Leif said, with a slight smile. 'When I first got into the game, I bought a healing-stone from a wise-woman who was retiring. It's a pretty good one, good against everything up to about level five wounds and level six disease.'

Megan blinked, apparently impressed. 'Level five? Anything that can grow back a chopped-off arm or leg must make you pretty popular on the battlefield. How the frack did you afford something like that?'

Leif laughed softly. 'Well, I shouldn't have been able to, really. But the lady was nice about it. I met her in the forest and she asked me for a drink of water, and I gave it to her—'

'Oh,' Megan said, 'one of *those* old ladies. You did her a Good Deed, and she Rewarded you.' There was a lot of this kind of thing in Sarxos: Rodrigues was not above pillaging old fairy tales, and folktales, and fantasy stories of any age, from the present time straight back to Lucian of Samosata, for familiar and unfamiliar themes. As a result, it was usually a good idea to treat strangers considerately when you met them in the woods. They might be players in disguise . . . or they might be the game's creator, interested in seeing if you were playing in the spirit he had intended.

'Well, rewarded, yeah, but she just gave me a discount. She didn't give me the thing for free,' Leif said.

'All the same, sounds like you got a bargain.'

'I did. It's as good a cover for me to go to Minsar as anything would be,' Leif said. 'There are probably a fair number of wounded who haven't been attended to yet, not by magic-workers, anyway. What's your excuse?'

'Same as usual,' Megan said. 'Freelance troublemaker – warrior, thief or spy, as necessary, and according to who'll pay me. I wander around, see who's doing what to whom, and sell the information to whoever's willing to pay the most. Do the occasional theft . . . in a good cause, of course. Fight, if it comes to that. Even here, where people should know better, they don't always suspect soon enough that a girl or woman may be as good a fighter as they are, or better.' She smiled, a slightly grim look. 'They suspect it even less when you don't look like a giant shieldmaiden with a brass bra and a big spear. That suits me fine: I don't mind exploiting archetypes . . . even if I'm only doing it negatively.'

Leif nodded, thinking. 'It's a good persona,' he said. 'Spies have a good reason to be anywhere . . . even when they don't, really. And they raise the level of paranoia around them just by being there. People let things slip that they might not have let slip otherwise . . .'

'Yup.' Megan drank more tea, paused for a moment to look down into her tankard. 'What the— There's something *in* this.'

'What? Extra herbs?'

'Herbs don't have this many legs. Just a bug,' Megan said, pausing for a moment to fish it out, examining it for a moment with a critical eye, and then tossing it over her shoulder. 'Okay. So you've got plenty of miles . . . we'll go after we finish here, then, if you're ready.'

'Yup. I need a few moments to make sure of the coordinates before we go, that's all. Don't want to wind up in Wussonia by mistake.'

Megan looked at him with a bemused expression. 'Wussonia . . .? I don't recognize the name.'

Leif grimaced. 'It's right over the other side of the Bay of Twilight,' he said. 'Little place. Isolated. With good reason.'

'Oh?'

'Don't look so interested! You wouldn't want to go there.' Leif shuddered slightly. 'The place is, well, it's on the soft side. Full of homesick princesses disguised as bards wandering around on quests for the Magic Whatsit, and wise telepathic unicorns with big eyes full of some ancient sorrow, and little tiny dwarfs with pointy hats that ride around on friendly forest animals. Miniature bears and badgers living in little houses built into the trunks of trees. Tiny fluttery fairies with gauzy wings.'

Megan made a face. 'Sounds like it would be bad for your blood sugar.'

'Or your sanity. It's not all that far from Minsar, that's the problem. Misplace a decimal point in the transit spell, and we could wind up there. Or, worse, in Arstan or Lidios.' He glanced again over at the guy who was, for the third or maybe the fourth time, cleaning his Glock-clone.

'No, thanks,' Megan said, 'there are enough guns where I live already . . .'

Leif nodded and sat back, stretching his legs out. 'Even if we're not already on the right track, which I doubt,' he said, 'we should be able to find out something useful up in Minsar, if as you say the big Players are converging on the place. The gossip always runs hottest after a battle . . . especially a battle where one of the protagonists got bounced.'

'That's what I'm counting on,' Megan said. 'If we can just— What *is* it?' she said curiously, for Leif was suddenly looking under the next table again.

'Uh oh,' Leif said. 'Well, I guess this has gone far enough. *Esmiratovelithoth—!*'

There was a BANG! of displaced air from under the table. Heads snapped up all around the room, most noticeably that of the guy cleaning the almost-Glock. Everyone stared.

From beneath the table, somewhat grimy, and swearing, the inn's landlord crawled. His face and arms were badly scratched. The marks looked like cat scratches, but seemed much deeper and wider than they should have. Muttering, but pointedly not looking at Leif, the landlord got to his feet, brushed himself off, and headed for the kitchen, swearing with constantly increasing fluency as he went.

The dark-cloaked man in the chimney corner was laughing, more at the guy with the Glock than at the innkeeper. Megan looked after the latter with interest. '*He* was that mouse?'

'Uh huh.'

'Doesn't that violate the square-cube law or something? I mean, what did he do with all that mass while he was mouse-sized?'

'Hey,' Leif said, 'it's magic, which means the software handles the sordid details. Don't ask me about software design . . . it's not my problem.'

They got up. Megan tossed a coin ringing to the table. The innkeeper's daughter swooped on it, bit it in the approved fashion, and stowed it away in her bodice. 'This one's on me,' Megan said, as the girl went away. 'Under the circumstances, you might get in trouble if you tried to pay. Guy might think you were putting a curse on him . . .'

'Now I would never do a thing like that.'

'Tell *him*,' Megan said, glancing back at the glaring, swearing innkeeper.

They made their way out.

★　★　★

Megan was just as glad to be leaving, as a fight had begun brewing between the Glock guy and the dark-cloaked man sitting close to the fireplace. 'You lookin' at me?' the Glock guy was demanding. 'Nobody else here to look at, you lookin' at *me*?'

'Gonna be lively in there in a few minutes,' she said, as she and Leif headed toward the big square of grass that was the 'village green' in front of the Pheasant and Firkin.

'Better to get away now, then,' Leif said. 'More interesting stuff's going on in Minsar, anyway. By the way, when we get there, do we "know each other"?'

Megan thought about that as they made their way through the evening dark to an empty patch of grass across from the tavern. Here and there, in the grass, sheep were grazing, and they had left in the grass the kind of thing sheep frequently leave behind them, so that Megan watched where she put her feet. 'I don't see why we shouldn't. There are enough chance meetings in Sarxos that no one's likely to suspect anything in particular. And neither of us is high-profile enough to attract any attention by being in the other's company.'

'Right,' Leif said. 'OK, we can make the transit from here.'

'Not there,' Megan said, pointing at the ground. 'Unless you want to bring that big lump of sheep-byproduct with us.'

'Oh.' Leif moved over a few feet. 'Right.'

'How big is the transit locus?' Megan said.

'Five feet. Ready? Here we go.'

Megan looked around her to make sure nothing she needed was outside the five-foot locus. Nothing was: her weapons were all very closely fastened to her person, the ones that weren't already part of her.

Leif said a sixteen-syllable word.

The world went black, then white, then dark again, and Megan's ears popped hard: then a few seconds later, popped again, while she was still trying to rub the dancing phosphene-dots out of her eyes. The problem with these transit spells was that they briefly did the virtual-reality equivalent of popping you into and out of hyperspace, and left you disoriented and half-blind for some seconds, as if someone had blown off a flashbulb in your face.

Megan blinked. Her vision was returning fast. They were standing in the profound stillness of a thick dark pine forest, of the kind which appeared in entirely too many fairy tales, and night was coming on fast. The city of Minsar was nowhere to be seen.

'You missed,' she said, trying hard not to sound too accusatory.

'*Merde*,' Leif muttered, 'stinking damn *du tonnere*, how'd *that* happen?'

'I wouldn't worry about it,' Megan said, restraining herself to keep from laughing. She knew Leif was good with languages, but this was not the kind of use she normally pictured such a talent as being put to. 'Let's just find out where we are.'

'Yeah, right . . .' Leif looked around him, then put his fingers to his mouth and whistled, piercingly.

Megan watched with slight envy. Even with three

brothers, this was one talent she had been unable to master. Her teeth were apparently just in the wrong places relative to one another. Leif whistled again, louder; then looked around, expectant.

There was a rustling in a pine tree near them. Something black dropped from a higher branch to a lower one.

It was a pathfinder bird. The birds were positioned here and there around the game as general advice-givers. In Sarxos, if nowhere else, you could safely claim, when someone asked you about something, that 'a little bird told you . . .' Some of them were not so little. This one was the size and color of a crow, but it had an intelligent and slightly nasty look which few crows could have mastered.

'Hey,' Leif said, 'we need advice.'

'Just got a fresh supply in this morning,' said the bird, in a rather smarmy voice which suggested that it had been a used car dealer in a previous life. 'If you turn off here and take *that* road for a mile or so—' and it pointed off to the left with its beak – 'you'll find before you, on a high peak, a fair maiden lying on the rock, surrounded by fire—'

'*Oh*, no, no way,' Leif said hurriedly. 'I know how *that* one ends. Nuclear war would be preferable.'

'You sure wouldn't get as much singing afterwards,' Megan said. 'Bird, which way is Minsar from here?'

The bird eyed her coolly. 'What's it worth to you?'

'Half an English muffin?'

The bird considered. 'You're on.'

Megan rooted around in her pack and came up with

it, beginning to crumble it onto the ground. The bird flew down and began pecking at the bits, but Megan took a step forward and shooed it away.

'Hey!' said the bird, aggrieved.

'Directions first,' said Megan.

'Stay on this road for a mile and a half, take the first left, hold that for a mile and a half and you'll be at the fords,' the bird said. 'The city's two miles north of there. Now gimme.'

Megan stepped back, and the bird fluttered forward. 'I tell you, it ain't like it used to be,' it muttered as it started gobbling the muffin crumbs. 'No trust, that's the problem. Nobody trusts anybody any more.'

Leif chuckled. 'Nobody gets anything for nothing, here, you mean,' he said. 'Bye bye, birdie.'

The bird, busy stuffing its face, didn't answer.

They walked away. Leif still looked a little put out at having messed up his first transit. 'I can short-jump us from here,' he said. 'Coordinates shouldn't be a problem.'

Megan shrugged. 'Why use up good miles when we're so close? We might as well walk. It's not like the forest's haunted, or anything.'

'I haven't heard that it is,' Leif said. 'But still . . .'

'If you want to jump, okay,' Megan said. 'But a few miles in the dark doesn't bother me.'

'Oh, well . . . you're right, I guess. Come on.'

They walked. Getting to Minsar took them something over an hour, and they heard and smelled the place long before they saw it. It was not the city proper they smelled first, though. It was the battlefield, down by the fords.

Subjective time in Sarxos passed more slowly than it did in the real world. Rodrigues had apparently intended this from the beginning, both as a way for his players to get more experience for their money, and as a punning reference to the old legends about the way time was supposed to go more slowly for those taken away by elves or other supernatural beings into the Otherworlds. This meant that it might have been a week and a half in the outside world since Shel Lookbehind's battle with Delmond, but here only a few days had passed. And not even a whole army of scavengers could have cleaned up the Fords of Artel by now. It being well after dark, the carrion birds were gone. But as Leif and Megan walked down to the fords, and their footsteps crunched on the gravelly strand, many glinting eyes looked at them from across the river, curious, their feasting disturbed.

'It's just wolves,' Leif said.

Megan gritted her teeth, as much at the smell as at the sight of all those interested eyes as the two of them waded across through the cold swift water. '*Just?* Just about a hundred of them.'

'Smells like they've got plenty to keep them busy,' Leif said. 'They won't bother us.'

'Nope,' Megan said softly. Leif glanced at her, and looked slightly surprised at the length and sharpness of the knife which had suddenly appeared in her hand.

'Where'd you have that?' he said.

'Out of sight,' Megan said, as they made their way

through the middle of the battlefield – there was no use trying to go around it. Bodies were everywhere. The eyes watched them as they passed, then became interested once again in their grisly meals. In the silence of the night, the wet sound of flesh being eaten and bones being chewed was loud.

Megan was very glad when they finally got up to the road, and the noise faded away behind them, around a curve. The smell took rather longer to wane: and by the time it was gone, they were already smelling Minsar's sewage system, which dumped the run-offs from the gutters down the centres of its streets into pools out beyond the walls.

Minsar was several hundred years old, and had outgrown its walls twice. Around the outsides of the old granite-block walls was a more or less permanent town of tents and shanties, and the inevitable little crowd of industries too foul-smelling or dangerous to be allowed to do business inside the walls, like the tanners and papermakers, and the bakers (like other cities, Minsar had discovered that, under the right conditions, flour could become a high explosive.) Now, though, there was a new ring of tents and temporary structures outside the 'outer ring:' the pavilion and wagons of the army which had defended Minsar, and several other groups of warriors, large and small, who had come there under the auspices of one lord or another to check the situation out.

Megan and Leif made their way toward the city gates through a maelstrom of noise and ferocious odors. Roasting meat, spilled wine, baking bread (the bakers were apparently working twenty-four hours a day to meet the increased demand), horses and horse dung, the stinking stagnant pools under the city walls, the occasional drift of perfume from some passing camp-follower or newly scrubbed-and-scented soldier just out of the bathhouses built outside the walls, all their smells wove together among the sound of the many voices speaking or shouting in many languages, laughing, cursing, joking, talking. Leif and Megan listened to the talk as best they could as they made their way to and through the gates.

The gate-wardens were keeping only the slackest watch. The town was plainly still in holiday mood after being saved from being sacked by Delmond. Most of the talk around Leif and Megan, as they made their way down the cobbled open space of the main street, was about that: the narrow escape, the army suddenly without its leader, and what would happen to that army now.

'Where'd the knife go?' Leif said softly.

'Away,' Megan said.

'Good. Knives are illegal in here.'

'Don't think anyone'll be able to enforce the statute tonight,' Megan said, looking around at the hordes of armed men and women milling around, trying to get into the town-square taverns, or spilling out of them with drinks in hand. She found herself trying not to stare at one gaudily dressed hunchbacked dwarf who crossed her path, pushing his way through the crowd and waving a miniature sword, to the guffaws of others. '*You* want to try taking the swords off all these people? How many watchmen do you think there *are* in Minsar?'

'Tonight? Fewer than usual,' Leif said. 'I take your point—'

They drifted past another crowd outside a tavern door. Inside was an impossible crowd, packed together like medieval sardines, shouting and pushing to get to the bar or to get away from it. A burly beermaid was pushing through the crowd with double handfuls of beermugs, made not of glass or ceramic, but of leather, tarred inside. She was using the leather 'jacks' as effective offensive weapons, and there was a small clear space around her as people backed off to avoid being splashed or trampled.

Leif drifted into the crowd outside the door and burrowed into it a little way, and Megan followed him: the rush of voices closed over her head like water over a swimmer.

'—don't know why Ergen insists on coming in at night when it's going to be the most crowded—'

'—get out of here—'

'—up in the big hall looking for Elblai, she didn't stay there long, so I thought—'

'—too many idiots in here looking to get drunk and start a brawl, I wouldn't—'

'—five malts and a burned-wine—'

Megan watched one of the earlier speakers head out of the crowd, followed by a couple of friends. She nudged Leif, gestured him away.

He nodded, followed her a little way out of the press. 'It's a pity they don't have showers here,' he muttered.

'I feel like I need one after that.'

'Hey, the night is young. Listen, I heard a name I know.'

'Oh?'

'Yeah. "Elblai." See those guys? Going down that little lane. Come on.'

He looked around, located them in the crowd: two tall men, two smaller ones and one who was very short indeed, heading off down a street which was more the size of an alley. Megan headed on after them.

Leif followed. 'What did they say?'

'Just something that made me feel nosy.' She smiled slightly in the torchlit dimness. 'When you spy long enough, you get hunches about what's worth listening to. This could be something—'

Megan turned into the lane, with Leif behind her. The lane was no more than four feet wide, with shuttered doors and windows on both sides. 'This isn't a street,' Leif muttered, 'it's a walk-in closet—' Down at the end of the lane, one door was open a crack: the flicker of firelight streamed through it, and from inside came the mostly shut-in sound of more talk, laughter, shouting.

The door opened wider to let in the men who were ahead of them, then started to close again. Megan pushed forward to follow them before the door closed completely. She squeezed through, trying to make it look casual. Inside, there was a fireplace directly across from the door, and beside it a hatch leading through into the kitchen. The hatch had a broad sill with several pitchers of beer waiting on it and, as Megan and Leif came in, hands poked out through the hatch and handed a passing server a roast chicken on a plate. This was apparently a moderately classy place: where other taverns might have had torches stuck in iron brackets in the walls, this one had real lamps, oil lamps with glass in them. On the old scarred tables scattered around there were rushlights, each rush clamped into a little iron holder and burning like a small smoky star. Most of the tables were full of people eating and smoking and drinking and talking.

Leif, behind Megan, nudged her, indicating an empty table off to one side, not too close to the one being taken by the men they had followed in, not too far away to make their conversation inaudible. Fortunately, the men seemed to have no concern about inaudibility. They shouted for the tavernkeeper, ordered wine, settled down around their table, and picked up their conversation more or less where it had left off.

'—just go away like that.'

'He got bounced. Everybody knows that.'

'Yeah, well, are they sure it's genuine?'

'Oh, come on, whoever heard of anyone faking a bounce? I don't think it can be done. The Rules.'

'Don't know that there's anything in the Rules against it,' said the smallest man, a fellow with a hawklike face and small wise eyes. 'Might be an interesting new tactic. Vanish . . . then come back where you're not expected.'

Megan was distracted as a tall, slender woman stopped by their table and said, 'Whaddayawant?'

'Your best honeydraft, good woman,' Leif said. 'And for my companion—'

'*Gahfeh*, please,' Megan said. 'Morstofian roast, thick cream, double sweet.'

The tall slender woman tossed her long dark hair back and said, 'No cream. Double sweet's extra.'

'Oh well, no cream, single sweet,' Megan said, resigned. The woman went away, making a face that suggested Megan's sanity was in question for asking for extras.

'. . . Think that's a tactic I'd care to try,' said one of the men. 'And it doesn't sound like Shel, either.'

'Oh, you know him well, do you?'

'No, but I hear the stories the same as everybody. If he—'

They broke off as the serving-woman came to their table, and there was a long digression mostly involving hot and cold drinks. Megan wasn't interested in that, but she was interested in the reaction of some of the other people, warriors and merchants both, who were sitting near enough to hear what was going on. Some of them were leaning in the men's general direction while trying to look as if they weren't. When the serving-woman went away, the men to whom Megan had been listening had dropped their voices considerably. She frowned a little and became interested in her *gahfeh*, which had just arrived.

'Nasty theory,' Leif said under his breath.

'Sometimes people can't stand believing what's really happened,' Megan said. 'They start rationalizing. I wish they'd mention that name again, is all.'

Leif shook his head, a 'what's the use' gesture. One of the men's voices was growing louder. '—Why we should be slumming it down here when the rest of them are up in the great hall.'

Megan found herself wishing that this were not a game, but some more mundane form of entertainment that you could simply turn up so as to hear better. 'No way they'll let us in there,' said the man to whom the first one was talking.

There was another pause as their drinks arrived. The first man lifted the leather jack with the ale he had ordered, took a long swift drink from it. 'Not us maybe, but all the big Players, they're all gettin' in, they can't afford to piss anyone off up there tonight. Who knows who might turn up, not get in, go away angry . . . and turn up next week with five thousand people that nobody here'll dare turn away? The city's picking up the bill for executive entertainment tonight, I'll bet. In their best interests. Tomorrow, who knows, they might run out of food and have an excuse to throw everyone out. But nobody's gonna throw the big guys outa there, not tonight. Too many deals brewing.'

'Aah, what would *you* know about deals?'

'Oh, I know, all right . . .'

'Yeah, you're Argath's best buddy, I know all about it. That's why you're down here with the rest of us, drinking this watered stuff.'

There was laughter, and a growl which suggested that it might turn nasty if the others kept teasing its owner. Leif looked over at Megan.

'You heard a name? What name?' he said.

She told him.

'Well,' he said, 'I think we just heard another one. Sounds like it might be worth a visit.'

'Yeah, sure, if we can find a way to sneak in there without getting tossed out on our ears.'

Leif looked thoughtful. Megan sat quiet for a few seconds – the chat at the other table had dropped out of audibility again as a couple of men tried to calm down the one who had sounded ruffled – and then said very softly to Leif, 'How good a hedge-wizard *are* you?'

He looked at her with slightly affronted professional pride. 'Pretty good.'

'Want to do another transit?'

'What, from *here*? Miss a decimal place and we'll both wind up inside a wall, and there go a couple of perfectly good characters. And this whole mission. No thanks!'

'Okay. Can you do invisibility?'

Leif looked at her, slightly surprised. 'Of course.'

'For two?'

He thought about that. 'Not for long.'

'It doesn't have to be. Just long enough to get us into the main hall where the bigwigs are having their meeting. After that we can hide behind a tapestry or something.'

'This is going to cost me points,' Leif said.

'It's in a good cause. Oh, come on, Leif, I'll transfer you some points to cover what we use! I'm not short of score myself.'

'Okay,' Leif said. 'Let's get as close as we can, though. The great hall here is where?'

'In the central keep, I'm pretty sure.'

Leif nodded.

As casually as they could, they finished their drinks, paid their bill and headed out into the tiny lane, chatting in a way they hoped would sound normal: it was quiet people moving through the dark who would attract attention on a night like this. 'If they're both in there,' said Leif, 'we're in business.'

'*If* they are,' Megan said. They headed for the keep, a tall square stone structure that towered over the rear of the central marketplace-square.

Around its open front door were gathered what looked like part of several companies of bodyguards, drinking out of good metal cups and talking quietly while looking around them with at least some semblance of alertness. Most of them wore colored surcoats over their armor, and almost all of them had someone's badge embroidered on the surcoat-breast. They looked at Megan and Leif with only mild interest as they passed by, heading for the shadows off to the side of the keep, where a narrow road ran deeper into the city. As Megan passed, she got the briefest glance through the big door of what was going on inside: a whirl of color, voices muttering and echoing off the room's high ceiling, huge tapestries at the back of the room moving slightly in breezes from the high slit-windows they concealed.

Leif picked a spot just around the front corner of the keep, where the torchlight didn't fall, and felt around in one of his pockets. 'Game interaction,' he whispered to the air.

Megan felt the slight vibration in the air that told her the games computer was speaking to Leif so as not to be heard by anyone else. 'Points transfer,' he said. 'Invisibility. Locus for two.' He paused, and his eyebrows went up. He looked at Megan. 'Do you know how much this is going to—'

'I don't care, as long as it's not more than three thousand,' she said, 'because that's about all the points I've got.'

'Oh, no, it's only two hundred.'

'Fine. Game interaction,' she whispered.

'Listening,' said the computer softly in her ear.

'Transfer two hundred points to Leif.'

'Done.'

'Finished.'

'Okay,' Leif said. 'You know how this works?'

'Generally.'

'Don't get between anybody's line of sight and a strong light source,' he said. 'Fortunately it's going to be mostly just torches in there. Stay close to the walls, that's the best way, and if you do have to cross in front of light, do it low. Keep your voice real low. The locus amplifies sound. And for Rod's sake don't bump into anybody.'

'Right.'

'Game intervention,' Leif said.

A brief silence. 'Invisibility locus,' Leif said.

Suddenly everything was buzzing, and her skin itched. Megan looked around her. Everything else was normal, but when she lifted her hands in front of her eyes, she couldn't see them.

She turned, and found that she couldn't see Leif, either. This was a side-effect that she hadn't quite anticipated for some reason. 'Okay,' said his voice nearby, sounding unnaturally loud, 'look, I'm going to head in through the front door when the guards aren't paying too much attention to the space between them, and there's no one else going in or out. You do the same. Then I'll make for the nearest hiding place on the right side. You do the same, but cut left. Circulate for a while. Then pick out the biggest tapestry in the place and get behind it. I'll let the invisibility relax while we're there – it's a strain holding it too long.'

'Okay. But what if there's somebody behind the biggest tapestry already?'

'Pick the next biggest. And pray it isn't occupied too.'

They made cautiously for the big front door. Megan had to dodge quickly a couple of times as people brushed past her, nearly touching her. She had to do it a few times more as she stood in front of the open door, waiting for her moment. But finally there came a period of a few seconds when no one was going in or out, and the soldiers guarding the door were both looking in opposite directions.

She slipped in, bumping against something she couldn't see: Leif. It took her a moment to recover from the shock, and then she was through the door, ducking out of the way of an elegantly dressed noble-man who was coming right toward her. She held still just long enough to scan the room quickly. It was a nobly decorated place, for a chamber which had started out as just four bare walls and a lot of holes to put ceiling-joists in. Now there was a permanent ceiling, instead of the temporary one that would have been there when the keep was built strictly for defense: tall white polished pillars had been installed down the length of the room. A large patterned red-and-blue carpet ran down the middle of the room, and the skins of various beasts, mostly sheepskins, were scattered over by the far walls, where the tapestries hung to cover the bare stone and keep the drafts out. In the center of the room, people were scattered all over, mostly in small knots of three or four, drinking and talking. Down at the end of the room, in front of the biggest tapestry, was a dais – one hardly worthy of the name, really: it only went up one step – and on it was a white chair. The chair was empty.

That chair spoke, possibly more eloquently than anything else, of the situation here. The city of Minsar had no real owner, now: not since Shel was gone. Now its great hall was full of potential owners . . . people who were looking over the real estate, and some of whom were not what a real estate agent would have called 'time wasters.'

Megan looked around as she made her way cautiously over toward the left wall and pressed herself up against it to get her breath for a moment, and try to shake some of the buzzing out of her ears. She considered that it might be a bad time coming for Minsar. Unless the city could find itself a powerful protector, and soon, it would shortly find one or another of these people at its door, in front of an army, and the message

being delivered would be, 'Accept us as "protec-
tors" . . . or lose what you've got.' There was a chance
that its potential protector was somewhere in this
crowd. That, Megan suspected, was why this party was
being held. No city wanted to be on the outs with its
new owner, or to be accused of having offered him or
her inadequate hospitality, after the dust had settled.

She looked around the hall to determinate which was
the biggest tapestry. That was the one behind the
throne – no way around it. At least no one seemed to
be gathering there – a lot of people were looking at that
throne, from a distance, but no one was going too near
it. *Maybe nobody wants to look too eager, this early in the
proceedings*, Megan thought.

She stepped out cautiously and made her way slowly
along the left-hand side of the hall toward the dais,
listening carefully as she went. Up ahead of her was a
big spread of food laid out on a U-shaped array of
tables, and the noble guests were in the process of
descending on the buffet as if they hadn't eaten in days.
Strolling among them, trying to look casual – or so
Megan thought – was a man fairly plainly dressed in
dark gray, but with a thick golden chain around his
neck, its links the size of fists.

It was the mayor of the town, the only statutory
authority left in Minsar now that Shel was gone. To
Megan's eyes, the man had a rather harried expression,
despite his casual air: he was watching the guests with a
look that suggested he wasn't sure whether some kind
of fight over his town might not break out right here.
Fortunately, there was no sign of this. Megan looked

around at the nobles and high-caste warriors eating and drinking Minsar's food, and thought she saw people mostly intent on taking advantage of a good feed. What she didn't see, though, was the kind of clustering or circling of people which suggested that someone really important was there. She had learned to look for such little status-oriented gatherings, having come to recognize them from the occasional cocktail party her mother and father hosted: the rule was that the most important person at a party inevitably became the center of such bunches, though the people in the 'bunch' might cycle as the party went on. The other rule was that sooner or later, everybody ended up in the kitchen . . . though here, that was unlikely. The kitchen was strictly for the servants.

She passed as close to the buffet as she dared, listening hard, not daring to linger too close for fear someone should bump into her. It was dangerous business, invisibility. There were players who would react to feeling something they couldn't see with a knife.

'—the salmon's very nice—'

'—out of wine. Where *is* that girl? Place is shamefully understaffed—'

'—not worth my trouble, I think. It's on the small side, and the squabbling has started already.'

'Oh?'

'Of course. Just look around you. Anybody who's serious is off somewhere private, doing a deal. Though not with *him*, he's out of the loop—'

The person speaking, some kind of duke or baron to

judge by the small informal coronet, glanced at the Mayor, smiled, glanced away again. He then came right around the table toward Megan, heading for where a small suckling pig was laid out—

She backpedaled hurriedly to get out of his way. The duke or baron turned his back on her and picked up a handy knife.

Megan got well out of range. There were people who could sense invisibility, and it was better to be cautious, especially around knives, which could fly out of someone's hand without warning . . . as she knew very well. Megan moved as quietly as she could to the big tapestry behind the throne, and slipped behind it.

Well down behind it she could just see Leif. She assumed he could see her as well. He was carefully standing where the dais and tapestry would combine to keep anyone from seeing his feet. She moved down to join him.

'You see him out there?' she said.

'Huh— Oh, it's you. What?' Leif muttered.

'The mayor of the town,' she said. 'Buttering up the dignitaries. Literally.'

'Yeah.'

'Look, get this off me for now. This buzzing is a nuisance. I can't hear.'

'It's spell artifact,' Leif said, and instantly it went away as he relaxed the spell. 'No way to get rid of it without getting rid of the spell too. If you insist—'

'Not a chance,' Megan said hurriedly. 'I'm way underdressed for this crowd. And as for *you*, you look like you slept in a tree. Did you know that there's straw sticking out of your wizard's hat?'

'It's for atmosphere,' Leif said, sounding slightly injured. 'A hedge-wizard has to look like he's *been* in a hedge recently.'

Megan snickered, for Leif had *that* aspect of his persona handled. 'I'm going out once more,' she said. 'But this is really a pain. You can make yourself invisible again if you want, but I'm tempted to mug one of the serving-women and take her clothes and just walk around with a wine pitcher. It'd be easier to hear.'

Leif raised his eyebrows. 'It's your call. Anything yet?'

'Nothing but a suggestion that anyone we'd be interested in hearing is probably somewhere else.'

Leif grunted. 'I guess that's no surprise. Still— Meet you back here in a few minutes. You want the spell, or are you really going to mug that wench?'

She sighed. 'The spell.' A moment later the buzzing in her ears was back, and Leif was nowhere in sight. 'Thanks. See you in a bit.'

The tapestry billowed out slightly and he was gone. Megan went out the other side, watching most carefully where she walked. Invisibility was useful, but you had to have eyes in the back of your head, never knowing from what unexpected direction someone might approach, and it was *very* strange walking around without being able to see your feet.

She made for the buffet table again, and spent the next fifteen or twenty minutes becoming very adept at getting close to the food and the conversations without banging into anyone or getting banged into herself. She even started stealing food, very circumspectly. The salmon was very good, which was nice, since she was partial to it.

'—just about finished here, I think,' said a very simply dressed man in slashed and purfled midnight-blue.

The elderly woman he was talking to, with beautiful silvery hair pulled back tight, wearing an ornate dress in black and silver, said, 'Well, I suspect the place's fate will be sorted out within a few days, for better or worse. A pity: I kind of liked it as a pocket democracy. But someone will make a bid – probably as a result of the action coming on the Marches.'

'What, the *north* Marches? So close? And so soon? I would have thought this business would drag on for a few more weeks, at least.'

The elderly lady looked around her before replying. No one else was close – or seemed close – and she lowered her voice and said, 'Elblai has something up her sleeve, I think. I saw her going upstairs to talk to Raist . . . and without the man himself here, Raist would be doing the negotiating.'

'Argath's not here?'

'He left about an hour ago – I saw him myself. In a hurry, too. I think things may be coming to a boil . . . something going on with his armies that he needs that world-famous charisma to handle.'

'Leaving Raist Wry-mind to sort out the details?'

'I don't think Raist will be doing much sorting.' The old woman chuckled. 'My money's on Elblai . . .'

They moved away. Megan looked at the tapestry

behind the empty chair, saw it flutter, swallowed, and headed that way.

Behind the tapestry, Leif was scratching. 'The itch does really get to you,' he muttered.

'I wish you hadn't mentioned that,' Megan said, suddenly feeling like a walking ad for an anti-flea preparation. 'Look, I just heard something germane. Argath's not here.'

'He's *not?*' Leif paused, and then took a breath and started softly muttering something heartfelt in a language which Megan suspected was Nordic. The muttering did not sound like prayers.

'Listen, just put a sock in it for a moment, all right?' Megan said.

'All those miles wasted—'

'Don't start cheapskating on me now, Leif. There's no time for it. You know who *is* here?

'Who?'

'Elblai.'

He blinked at that. '*That* Elblai?'

'The same. She's upstairs somewhere, having a quiet talk with one of Argath's people, so I hear.'

'*Zaffermets,*' Leif said. 'Remember what that guy back in the tavern was saying—'

'Yes, and I'm not going to discuss it any further unless you tell me what language '*zaffermets*' is! I think you make some of these words up just to impress people. It's not like you don't already speak umpty-ump languages as it is—'

'It's Romansch,' Leif said idly, looking around him. 'Sursilvan dialect, I think. Look, I think I can manage one more bout of the no-see-um spell.'

'Are you sure?'

'Do you want to go eavesdrop on Elblai, or don't you?'

'Ohh—' Megan was deep in exasperation. 'Come on . . . we've got to find them.'

'Shouldn't be hard. Staying invisible, though—'

'Don't let it slip,' Megan said, 'whatever you do. Come on, the stairs are this way—'

The stairs were guarded, but that was no obstacle to them: the guards, though alert, were not invisibility-sensitive, and were in no position to guard against what they couldn't see or hear. Megan and Leif stole up between them and went silently up the stairs, which followed the left wall up to the second floor. Leif concentrated as best he could on holding the invisibility spell in place. He had paid for it, all right, as had Megan, but if you were careless, you could drop it, just as you might drop and break something expensive that you'd bought. And in this case, dropping the spell could be just as costly . . .

The second floor was open-plan, one big room with carved or fabric-covered screens positioned here and there in the northern fashion, to make temporary privacy for anyone using the space. More thick tapestries were positioned around the walls to cut the drafts from the slit-windows. Off to one side, Elblai sat in a large, ornate chair located in front of a carved screen, and a man sat on a smaller chair in front of her. He was a small man, slender, short-haired and short-bearded, dressed in dark clothes.

Leif moved cautiously in that direction, staying very close to the wall. Leif could hear the soft sounds of Megan following behind him. The lighting up here was subdued, and mostly in the middle of the room, from a pair of oil lamps on intricately wrought metal stands.

Leif decided not to go any closer than ten feet or so, and flattened himself against the tapestry, being careful not to move it. He could feel a soft flutter in the wool as Megan did the same, and they both spent a moment examining Elblai. *She's worth looking at*, Leif thought: fiftyish, a little on the stocky side, with close-cropped silvery-blond hair and a face rather at odds with the housewifely body. She had eyes that were set a little slanted, giving her face a slightly exotic look, and her eyes were large, and thoughtful, and the deepest blue that Leif could remember seeing – almost a violet color. She looked like somebody's grandmother . . . but a grandmother sitting comfortably with a sword in one hand, point down on the stone floor, and wearing a beautiful glittering shirt of scalemail over a long padded silk tunic the color of the very tip of a candle flame. Her well-worn boots were up on a hassock in front of her chair, and she sat back in the chair holding her sword with one hand resting on the hilt, tilting it a little to one side, a little to the other, in a slow rocking motion as she talked.

'Those three have been a thorn in my side for months now,' she was saying in a soft Midwestern drawl to the small, dapper man sitting across from her.

'Now, your master is in a position to do me a good turn.'

'I am sure he could be convinced to do you one,' said the man, stroking his close-cropped beard, 'assuming that you could demonstrate to him that such an intervention would be to his advantage.' He was dressed all in shimmering black: quilted satin, another tunic meant to be worn under mail: but the mail had been laid aside, and he wore only a long dagger at his belt.

Elblai laughed out loud. 'Raist, you can't tell me that Lillen and Gugliem and Menel haven't been just as much pains in *his* butt as they are in mine. Since spring they've been wandering around the North country looking for a fight to interfere in. I didn't have anything going on that I wanted them interfering in, and I told them so, and told them to clear on out before I lost my patience. Well, they cleared out, all right, but where do they go? Straight off to the Orxenian marches, and what do they do but sell off their armies' contracts to Argath.'

'Oh, now,' said the dapper little man, 'now then, Lady Elblai, but you have your facts somewhat confused. Those contracts were purchased by Enver, Lord of the Marchlands, who as we all know—'

'—who as we all know doesn't fart without Argath telling him what color to do it in,' Elblai said, with an impatient frown. 'Don't insult my intelligence by trying to convince me that Enver is some kind of loose cannon. Argath instructed him to buy those contracts on the quiet, and point those three lords' armies at *mine*, which I might add have been sitting in summer quarters and very peaceably minding their own business. A state of affairs which your master cannot understand, and so believes that there must be some kind of plot behind it.'

Elblai uncrossed her legs and crossed them the other way, all the while rocking the point-down sword idly and gently back and forth, back and forth, so that it caught the light of one of the oil lamps, and the reflection slid back and forth over a hanging tapestry there, and the running hunting dogs on the tapestry seemed to stare at the moving patch of light. 'Well, he wants a plot, I'll give him a plot. Don't think I haven't noticed the troop movements the last few days. I know an encirclement when I see it. *Attempted* encirclement. Your master Argath had better look east, because my reinforcements are coming up, in force. And there are more than three times as many of them as he can field just now. I know his numbers, and his intentions, if he doesn't know mine. But that's what I hire my wizards for, and I make sure I have the best.'

The small dapper man sat very still. His face showed no change of expression at all.

'Now your master has several possible courses of action,' Elblai said, reasonably. 'He can go on the way he's going. In which case, late tomorrow or early the day after, Lillen, Gugliem and Menel are going to be fertilizer, along with their armies. And having put *them* to their best possible use, I'll then turn my attention to doing the same for Argath. It might take a little longer, but my people are mobilized and ready, and his are scattered all over the place, supposedly cowing the surrounding kingdoms into inaction. Well, we'll see about that. My guess is that the minute somebody attacks Argath with a force big enough to make a difference, then all the neighbors, who have been putting up with his depredations for quite long enough now, will join in, too. You think he fancies an attack on *five* fronts? Because that's what we're looking at. If not more. Argath King of the Orxenians will be a red greasy smear on the ground by the time my horse and everybody else's finishes up with running all over him.'

Elblai paused. There was utter silence in the room, except for the tiny, tiny noise made by the point of Elblai's sword as it grated on the stone floor. Leif held his breath, sure that someone would hear him breathing in that stillness. Beside him, he suspected that Megan was doing the same.

'Now,' Elblai said at last, 'that's one possibility. Another possibility is that he can call off his three little friends and tell them to take their armies somewhere else. In which case everyone will shortly know exactly what happened. None of them could ever keep a secret worth a damn, especially when they think they've been used for purposes which they didn't anticipate themselves. In this case, they'll sure think so, and your master will lose a lot of face, and lay himself open to all kinds of trouble, if not this year, then next. But I'd bet on this year, myself.'

'You are very certain of all this, aren't you?' asked Raist.

'Oh, you bet,' said Elblai. 'I'm equally certain that your master will not avail himself of possibility number two, either. Too much chance that he'll come out of it looking bad. So there is also possibility number three . . . in which he comes down on Lillen and Gugliem and Menel *himself*, and wipes their armies out – thus giving his army something to do besides be wiped out by mine – and makes a reputation for himself by 'keeping order in the Marches.' He gets to look good for a change. A nuisance, by which I mean those three and their armies, is removed. And Argath doesn't lose any face.'

Raist opened his mouth. 'But he wouldn't normally take possibility number three, either, I don't think,' Elblai said, 'because *he* didn't think of it first.'

Raist closed his mouth again. 'He'd probably have to kill Lord Enver, too,' Elblai added, as an afterthought, 'but he's been wanting to do that for a while anyway.'

There were a few breaths' more quiet. 'So,' Elblai said. 'You go back to your lord – he left an hour ago, heading north for his army's encampment – and explain the options to him. Be nice about it. I really prefer the third one, myself. But if he tries to force the issue, I am prepared to wipe him and his armies off the face of Sarxos, and not even Rod will shed a tear. You just have him to be clear about that, because I always like to have one good fight before the autumn sets in . . . and if he insists, it'll be him. This is his last chance to change his mind, make it a nice quiet autumn for everybody . . . and ensure that he lives long enough to have one.'

Raist stood up. 'If I have your ladyship's permission to go—'

'In one moment more. I know, too, that after this campaign he has designs on Lord Fettick and Duchess Morn. Their countries have been in fairly precarious positions up until now. Well, we've been talking . . . and they're preparing to enter into a strategic alliance with another power – not me: let your lord and master do a little digging – who is eager to take him on. When that alliance is in place – within a matter of days, I'd think – the forces they're going to be able to bring into the field are going to be massive. They will almost certainly go straight to war, eager to get Argath out of their collective hair. And they'll take out Duke Mengor as well. They're perfectly aware to what use Argath has been putting *that* cooperative little puppet. So just have him understand that his troubles are just beginning.'

Raist stood there fidgeting, silent. After a moment, Elblai nodded at him. 'Go on, then. Be careful on the road. There are a lot of wolves running loose around here at the moment . . .'

Raist bowed hurriedly and left, his footsteps echoing down the stairs.

Elblai sat quietly in the still room. After a moment there were more footsteps on the stairs, and a young blond woman in a long, simple blue robe appeared on the landing. 'Aunt El?' she called.

'Over here, honey.'

Aunt? Leif thought.

The young woman came in. 'So?' she said.

Elblai sighed and leaned the sword against the arm of her chair. 'He's going to attack,' she said. 'I'm pretty sure.'

99

'So what're you going to do?'

Elblai got up and stretched. 'I'm going to run him and his troops right into the ground,' she said. 'I don't see that I'm going to have much choice, if I'm to sustain my position. As for him, I'd prefer to avoid the killing, but he hasn't got the brains Rod gave Blue Point oysters, and he *will* insist on doing the showy thing. Won't help him, not this time.'

The young woman sighed, almost exactly the sound her aunt had made. 'All right,' she said. 'I'll talk to the other captains and update them, and we'll send out messengers to the reinforcements.'

'Do that. Tell them I think Argath will try to scrape together some more troops from the tributary kingdoms. I don't think he can find many more than a couple thousand extra, though, not at this short notice. We're still going to outnumber him three to one – which is just the way I like it. Never had time for these even-steven death-or-glory stands, myself.' She snorted – a sound Leif had heard from his own grandmother, occasionally, so that he smiled. 'Let's get that seen to . . . and then go down and have some dinner before everybody eats it all.'

They went out.

Once again, Leif relaxed the invisibility spells. To their relief, the buzzing in their ears subsided.

Leif glanced sidewise at Megan.

'We've got a big problem,' Megan whispered.

'Yeah? Yeah?'

'Keep your voice down. Weren't you listening? She's

going to take Argath,' Megan said. 'That makes her a prime target for being bounced.'

Leif looked at her cockeyed. 'Wait a minute. *You* were the one who was going on before about not theorizing without data. We don't have any more data than we did before . . . except some about an attack that's about to happen.'

'Sure . . . but you heard it, Leif! She's got Argath outnumbered three to one. She's going to cream him. And it's people who've creamed him in the past who've gotten bounced.'

'Listen, I hope she *does* cream him,' Leif whispered. 'He's not exactly an example of high Sarxonian moral standards, is he? And besides, if his character gets killed, and people still get bounced, then maybe we have some evidence that it's not him doing it.'

Megan stared at him. 'That would be as circumstantial as what we've got now,' she said. 'Leif, if Elblai *is* going to be attacked somehow, and we suspect it, we've got to go out on a limb a little and let her know about it! She's got a tremendous character running here – it wouldn't be fair to let her be bounced just for the sake of tempting the bouncer out into the open. She's got to take some precautions.'

'If we *do* warn her,' Leif said, 'it could warn off Argath, or whoever's responsible for these bounces. And we'll lose a chance to find out who he or she is.'

Megan clutched her head. 'I can't believe we're having this argument. You can't just use another player as bait!'

'Megan, think straight for a moment! Warn her *how*?

We don't know who she is in real life, and we're not going to find out. What about the confidentiality rules? If she's secret, and chooses to be, there's no way we can find her.'

'If we got hold of the gamesmaster,' Megan said, 'through Net Force—'

'Sure. Ask them to break confidentiality on a suspicion? No way they'll do it.'

'We'll have to go warn her now, then,' Megan said.

Leif looked at her for a long moment. Then, rather reluctantly, he said, 'All right. You saw her device – that basilisk. There were a few of her people downstairs wearing it. Let's go down and introduce ourselves . . . come out in the open about it.'

'Right.'

Leif let go of the invisibility, relieved that he didn't have to hold it any more, and they went back downstairs again. In the great hall, they looked around, but there was no sign of Elblai herself.

'There are some little private rooms off the sides,' Leif said. 'She might be in one of those—'

'No,' Megan said. 'They'd be guarded. But look there.'

It was the young woman whom they had seen with Elblai earlier. Over her plain blue robe she had thrown a darker one, with the rampant basilisk badge of Elblai's people on it. She was looking thoughtfully around the room at the nobles and warriors as they ate and drank and talked.

They went over to her, causing some interest and amusement among the assembled nobles as they took in the sight of the somewhat oddly dressed party crashers. 'Excuse me,' Leif said to the young blond woman, and bowed slightly. 'If, as I think, you are with the noble lady Elblai—'

'If you're looking for an audience,' said the woman, eyeing him with an interested expression, 'I'm afraid she is not available tonight.'

'Not an audience,' Megan said softly. 'A warning.'

The woman put her eyebrows up. 'Of what?'

'Argath,' Leif said.

The woman's expression became much more guarded.

'If, as rumor has it, your lady is contemplating an attack on Argath's forces,' Leif said, 'we must warn her that something . . . unfortunate . . . might befall her afterwards. People who have beaten Argath in battle recently have been coming to harm . . . as we see from this gathering tonight.'

The expression on the face of Elblai's niece began to get downright chilly. 'An interesting warning,' she said. 'Who sent you?'

Leif opened his mouth, closed it again.

'One might think that such a warning would be to Argath's advantage,' the young woman said, 'if indeed any such attack were in prospect.'

'No one has sent us,' Megan said. 'We're working independently . . . and we mean your aunt the Lady Elblai nothing but good.'

The young woman's eyes widened just a very little, then hardened down again. 'That relationship is not widely known,' she said. 'Who *are* you?'

'Uh,' Megan said.

'We're investigating the bounces,' Leif said, and Megan felt a sudden rush of relief that he hadn't added 'for Net Force': that would have been going a little too far. 'We're afraid that your aunt is in danger of becoming a "bouncee" if she keeps going the way she's going.'

'Oh? And which way would that be?'

How do I put this the most diplomatically? Leif thought, wondering how his father would phrase this. *Probably pretty elliptically.* 'If Lillen and Gugliem and Menel—' Leif began.

The young woman's eyes narrowed right down. 'One does not normally speak of – external things,' she said, 'to people one doesn't know, and whose *bona fides* can't be guaranteed.' Her expression was quite chilly now. 'I think I must ask you to leave.'

'Please – just let us have a word with Lady Elblai—'

'That is impossible. She has been called away on business, which perhaps is fortunate.'

'Look, it's really important—' Megan said.

'Perhaps it is, to you,' said the young woman coolly. 'I would take your warning more kindly if it did not seem obvious that you, or someone connected with you, had recently been spying on us. Spies' advice has two edges, they say, and it's my business to protect my aunt against those who would do her harm.'

'But that's what we're trying to—'

'Good night,' the young woman said firmly. 'Leave right now . . . before I have you removed.'

They looked at her – then headed for the door.

Leif looked over his shoulder at the woman one last

time as they headed out. Elblai's niece had beckoned over someone else wearing her aunt's badge, a tall balding man, and was now whispering urgently in his ear. He looked after Leif and Megan, and then left the great hall hurriedly, out one of the side exits. Megan and Leif were still standing out in the roil and turmoil of the town's main square when a rider went by them at some speed – and then simply vanished with a clap of displaced air.

'Great,' Leif muttered. 'Now there's no way to tell *where* she's gone off to.'

'I'm getting a very bad feeling about this,' Megan said. 'I think this business with Argath has just heated up somehow. Otherwise, why would he be gone, too?'

Leif shook his head. 'Well,' he said, 'at least we tried.'

'Trying doesn't get the job done,' Megan said gloomily. '*Doing* it does.'

Leif looked at her wryly as they walked through the square. 'Ah, the classics again,' he said. 'Emerson? Ellison?'

'My mom,' Megan said. 'Come on . . . let's get out of here. We need to think, and, as much as I hate to say it, I always think best offline.'

They logged out of the game and went off to Leif's workspace. It was something Megan had only seen in pictures, a stave-house in the old Icelandic style, completely covered with shake shingles, and its steep gables sporting elaborately carved dragon-heads. Inside, the place was very clean and plain, done in a high-tech version of New Danish Modern, the big polarized windows looking out on a landscape of green rolling fields overarched by a high, pale blue sky.

Megan wasn't in much of a mood to enjoy the surroundings or the scenery. She and Leif argued for about an hour over what they'd done and how they could have done it better. At least, it turned into an argument: though that hadn't been her original intention.

'I'm not sure *how* we could have done it better, frankly,' Leif said. 'It was a fact-finding mission. Fine: we found facts. And pretty good ones, too.'

'Yeah . . . but, Leif, we're not going to be able to find out anything *fast* enough to do us any good! I can't get rid of the feeling that we should have gone about this in a more structured way . . .'

'Oh? And how long have you had this feeling? I don't think you had it before we left.'

'Whatever. I have it now. And I'm worried about those other two Elblai mentioned, too. Fettick and Morn.' Megan was pacing up and down, shaking her head. 'Supposing that Argath manages to walk away from this fight that's coming – which he might manage to do. He's got a pretty good record of escaping from trouble even when his whole army gets massacred – and then he decides to come down on them? From what Elblai said, they're going to be in a position to beat him as well . . . and that's going to make *them* potential "bouncees".'

'It will,' Leif said, 'if we're not running down a blind alley with this whole line of reasoning to start with . . .'

'If you've got anything better,' Megan said, 'I'd really like to hear it.'

Leif sat down on a severely plain couch and ran his fingers through that red hair in a gesture that said he didn't have anything else at all. 'Look,' he said, 'let's take a break from this, huh? We're just spinning our wheels.'

Megan sighed and nodded. 'Okay,' she said. 'Look, when should we meet again?'

'Maybe tomorrow night?' Leif said.

'Can't,' Megan said. 'Tomorrow night's a family night at our place: I don't game then. I get to watch my brothers sit and eat us out of house and home. The night after?'

'You're on.'

Megan prepared to tell her implant to exit. 'Look,' she said. 'Sorry I yelled at you.'

'No, you're not,' Leif said, and grinned, though the grin was crooked.

'All right. I'm not. But you were right, anyway. We did the best we could, to start with.'

Leif stuck one finger in his ear as if to clean it. 'Must be how long I had to hold that invisibility spell,' he said. 'I could have sworn you said I was right.'

'I'll say something else in a moment,' Megan said. 'And in English. See you the night after next.'

Leif waved at her as she vanished.

Megan blinked and found herself sitting in the chair in the office. The lights in the room were way down. She glanced over at the clock. It was very late, for a school night anyway. Fortunately she had taken care of her schoolwork before she ducked into Sarxos to meet Leif. *All I need is Mom on my case as well . . .*

She got out of the chair stiffly. *I've really got to have another word with the move-your-muscles program. I feel like I've been in the same spot for hours . . .* Quietly she moved around the downstairs office, shutting off the parts of the computer that got turned off at night, and paused by the desk, where someone had, for a change, thoughtfully pushed some piled-up books out of the way of the optical implant pickup. *Dining with William Shakespeare . . . Understanding Chaos Futures . . . War in 2080 . . . The Knight, Death and the Devil . . .*

What is *he researching?* Megan thought, yawned, and went off to bed.

She came down early the next morning to find her father sitting at the kitchen table and staring at the stereo-video window hanging on the kitchen wall with a rather concerned expression. 'Isn't this something you do in your off hours?' he said, pointing at the window.

Megan, who was in the act of struggling to pull a sweater on over her shirt, finally got it pulled down into place and stared at the window. It showed the Sarxos logo, and behind that, stereo footage of a stretcher being hovered out of a flyer ambulance into an emergency room by paramedics in the usual rescue-orange coveralls with the blue LifeStar on the backs. '—Assault was said by the woman's niece, a fellow Sarxos player, to possibly be related to a feud or vendetta attributable to some other gameplayer. Ellen Richardson, who plays in the popular Sarxos virtual-reality role-playing game under the nickname "Elblai," was on her way to her job at the post office in

Bloomington, Illinois when a hit-and-run driver forced her vehicle off the road and caused her to crash into a utility pole. She was taken to Mercy Downtown Hospital, where she is reported to be in a coma. Her condition is described as "critical but stable—" '

The view changed to that of a woman in a lab coat reading from a prepared statement. '—The patient is not responding to stimuli at this time, but she has been scheduled for surgery at the earliest opportunity, and doctors presently give her a seventy-thirty chance of—'

'OhmiGod,' Megan said softly.

'You didn't know her, did you?' her father said.

She shook her head, unable to look away from the stereo window, now filled with the face of the young blonde-haired woman to whom she had been speaking not eight or nine hours ago. It was streaked with tears, and contorted with barely controlled rage. 'We received a warning,' she was saying, 'that if my aunt continued a certain line of action she was taking in the game, something unspecified but unpleasant might happen to her. My aunt discounted this warning. You hear a lot of this kind of thing during the course of gameplay, people trying to bluff you out of their path. No one had *any* idea that someone would—'

She choked with tears, turned away from the camera, waving it away with one hand.

Megan stood there, going hot and cold with terror.

We were too late. Too late.

What if—

—oh, no, what if somebody thinks that we—

She ran for the computer to call James Winters.

Chapter 3

When she caught him in his office, the blinds were drawn, and Winters was gazing down thoughtfully at an audio-stereo information pad on his desk. 'Yes,' he said, not looking up for the moment, 'I thought I'd hear from you shortly. How much do you know about what's happened?'

'I heard about the lady in Bloomington,' Megan said. 'Mr Winters, I feel so terrible – we were with her just last night—'

'So Leif told me,' Winters said. 'She didn't know you were there, though.'

'No.'

'Tell me something,' Winters said: and then held up a hand. 'No, wait a moment. Before we go on to that—' He glanced down at the pad again. 'I've got a note here from the hospital at Bloomington. She's going into surgery now. Most of her injuries aren't too serious. It's the usual problem with brain trauma, though. You can't tell how bad it is until the brain's had time to "register" the injury and react to it. She apparently has a case of that they call "contrecoup,"

111

where the brain hits the inside of the skull and bruises with the impact. If they can get the swelling to go down in time . . . she'll be all right. At least it doesn't seem as if she's in any imminent danger of dying.'

'Oh, God,' Megan said, 'we should have tried harder, we should have found some way to warn her anyway, we should have—'

'Yes,' Winters said, only a little dryly, 'hindsight does tend to be twenty-twenty. But in this case, you need to step back from the events a little bit and see if your judgment's being clouded by what's happened. I'll admit, it's shocking.'

He sighed, pushed the pad away. 'In any case, that's something else I want you to do: step right back from this whole business and let us handle it now. When it's just machinery involved, burglary, destruction of property, that's one thing. But when assault starts coming into it – in this case, vehicular assault with a deadly weapon – that's when it becomes no longer merely Net Force Explorer business. I value anything you can tell me, though, about your own suspicions.'

'Suspicions are all we've got,' Megan said. 'But I can't get rid of the idea that they would have been enough to save her.'

'Maybe so,' Winters said. 'Leif spent a while telling me about a character named Argath.'

Megan nodded. 'Just about anyone who's had a fight with him in the last three game-years, and beaten him, seems to have been bounced.'

'But you're not sure he's responsible.'

'I don't know any more. Yesterday I was really

suspicious, but . . . there wasn't enough data . . .'

Winter smiled a little grimly. 'There still may not be. We need to be rather Holmesian about this . . . Of course, when Net Force proper comes into it, we'll be able to get the Sarxos people to cooperate with us and release proper names, game-logs and other such information. Of course it'll still take due process . . . they never like letting proprietary stuff go easily . . .'

Megan said, 'Maybe if a player approached Chris Rodrigues . . .'

Winter said, 'We can't spend too much time with the "maybes" at this point. We'll do this one by the book. Anyway, from what investigation you've done so far, is there anyone else upon whom suspicion might genuinely be thrown?'

'Nobody who's obvious to us, no. The problem is that there are so very many players. Even if we could get at it, the database is so massive . . . I keep thinking that there must be some way to winnow through everybody . . . but I don't know what that would be. Lots of players would have characteristics that would match a possible motive for attack, but only one of them is responsible. You can't go around accusing innocent people just on the off-chance that they might be guilty . . .'

'There speaks a future operative,' Winters said, and there was a grim note of approval in his voice. 'Well. Megan, you're still in shock. It's understandable. Leif was, too. Let's part company for the moment. But I'd appreciate a written debrief from you in the next eighteen to twenty-four hours: something to brief our operatives with when we send them in. Make it as detailed as you can. In fact, I'd appreciate it if you'd speak to the Sarxos people and give us access to your game-logs from last night.'

Megan blushed hot at that. 'Mr Winters,' she said very softly, 'I think some of the things we said were construed as threats—'

'I heard Mrs Richardson's niece's statement,' Winters said. 'I understand you have some concerns about what might be your legal status in this situation. I think you know that you have my confidence. Should there be any legal repercussions, you know that we'll do everything we can to support you. Can anyone at your home alibi you for last night?'

Megan shook her head. 'Nobody except the Net itself,' she said. 'There's no faking your identity when you log in, after all. It's your brain, your body and your implant. And as for the rest of it—' She shrugged, and then added with just the slightest smile, 'I'm not sure how I would have driven from here to Bloomington, Illinois in time to run Elblai – Mrs Richardson – off the road with a car.'

'There is that,' Winter said, and cracked a small smile himself. 'Never mind. You're covered enough for the moment. Go on, go to school, and get that report done for me tonight, if you would. We'll be sending in operatives ASAP. Meanwhile, you should consider yourself relieved of responsibility for this business. But I want to thank you very much for your help so far. You've at least given us a lead to follow, you two, and some potentially useful theories.

Plus a much better strategic assessment than we could have managed on short notice. It's much appreciated. You put your money and your time on the line . . . and possibly, considering the nature of the person we seem to be hunting, your personal safety as well, if that person got any sense of who you were and what you were up to.'

'I don't think we were anywhere near him,' Megan said. 'Thanks anyway.'

She cut off the connection, thought a moment, then spoke to her implant and had it call Leif.

He was sitting in his workspace in the stave-house, looking profoundly depressed – an unusual expression for him. He glanced up as Megan appeared in his space.

'You talk to him?'

'Yeah.'

'We're off the case.'

'Yeah.'

Leif looked up at Megan sideways. '*Are* we off the case?'

'What do you mean? Of course we're off. He took us off.'

'And you're just going to sit back and let it be that way? Just like that?'

'Well.' Megan looked at him.

Leif got up and started pacing. 'Look,' he said. 'I don't want to sound unduly heroic or anything. I don't know about you, but I'm feeling a little bit responsible.'

'For what? *We* didn't run that lady off the road!'

'We tried to warn her. We did it wrong. She didn't

115

get it. Don't you feel responsible for that?'

Megan sat down on that severely plain couch and dropped her head into her hands. 'Yeah,' she said. 'I do. A lot. And I don't know what we can do about it, now that it's happened.'

'Not just give up,' Leif said.

'But, Leif, you heard Winters. He's taken us out of the loop. If they catch us—'

'How are they going to catch us? It's not like we're not Sarxos players. It's not like we don't have a right to be in the game when we want to. Isn't that so?'

'Yeah, but – Leif, if we do that, they're gonna know right away what we're doing!'

'Are they? But we're good little Net Force Explorers, aren't we?' Leif's grin popped out, and looked unusually mischievous for a moment. 'Who'd ever suspect *us* of disobeying orders? Intentionally, anyway.' Leif held his head high and looked for a moment impossibly noble, innocent, and dim.

Megan had to laugh at the sight of him. 'Not that they can *give* us orders,' Leif said. 'Suggestions, yes . . .'

'You are amazing,' she said.

'Thank you. *And* modest.'

'Oy,' Megan said.

'Look,' Leif said. 'Think about it. The reason we're lucky enough to be Net Force Explorers in the first place is because they saw something in us that was not the usual kind of behavior. A little more willing to swing out into the unknown, maybe. If we just give up now because we're told to—'

'If we were *in* Net Force, we'd *have* to do what we were told, Leif! Discipline—'

'Frack discipline,' Leif said. 'Well, I don't mean that. But we're *not* fully in. It gives us a little—'

'—latitude?' She scowled.

'Megan, I'm telling you, I'm right on this one. And you know I am. That's why you're making those weird faces at me. You should see yourself.'

She looked at him dubiously. It went right against her grain to ignore Winters's 'suggestion.' She understood his concern. She knew what her parents would say if she told them anything about this. But whether she planned to tell them anything about this, right this minute anyway, was another story. *Maybe later. But right now – I have to make a choice.*

'Well—' she said.

'And look,' Leif said. 'We've still got problems. Argath, or whoever, is still out there, and I bet he, she, they, or it—'

'He, for my money,' Megan said.

'—yeah – anyway, they're still targeting people. They're not yet identified. What about those other two lords that Elblai was mentioning? Fettick and Morn? To judge by what she was saying last night, they're likely to be the next targets. I mean, look at it, Megan! Whoever's doing this, they're not waiting around to hit someone who's beaten Argath any more. Whether it *is* Argath himself, or someone using some kind of weird cover—'

'What I still don't get is why anyone would do that . . .'

'A grudge,' Leif said. 'Or the attacker is crazy. Never mind . . . there's still time to work that out. But whatever the cause, *whoever* it is that's doing this . . . they've stopped being patient about it. They're hitting people before they actually fight Argath: when it just looks like there's a possibility they might beat him.'

'Yeah . . . All right. I see your point. So – what'll we do? Go try to warn them? Which kingdoms were in question?'

'Errint and Aedleia,' she said. 'I know them slightly. They're northern – neighbors of Orxen. I've got more than enough transit to get us there. We can be there tonight. Their battles weren't scheduled to happen right away. It's just possible that we can—'

'What? Get them not to go ahead with a campaign that they've been planning, and that they really want? That's gonna be a good trick.'

'We've got to try. We didn't try hard enough last night . . . and look what happened. You want to see them run off a road . . . or worse? And what about all the others who might shortly be in the same situation? There have to be other players who've been waiting their chance to take Argath on. After these guys, they'll be a threat, too. If we can find out what other players are eager to fight him, we may be able to find some other connecting strand, some line of data that'll lead us to whoever's doing this. And I want them,' Leif said softly. 'I want them.'

Megan nodded slowly. She did not often feel physically violent. Even when she managed to engineer situations which gave her an excuse, every now and then, to toss her brothers around, it was mostly enjoyment she felt, and amused satisfaction at the looks on their faces as she reminded them that life was not always predictable. But now . . . now she felt, uncharacteristically, like she wanted to hurt somebody. Specifically, whoever had sent Elblai into the hospital, pale, with an oxygen mask hiding her pretty, motherly face.

'Look,' Leif said. 'Do your briefing for Winters. Get that finished, leave it on timed-send in your computer, and get it off to him tonight . . . after we're already in Sarxos. Or after we've come out.'

'Leif, I can't tonight,' Megan said. 'I told you, I have this family thing—'

'This is an emergency,' Leif said. 'Isn't it? Can't you beg off just this once?'

She thought about that, thought about the concerned look on her father's face. 'Probably,' she said. 'I don't usually do this . . .'

'Come on, Megan. It's important. And it's more than just those other people.' He looked at her, intense. 'What are you really thinking about doing after you get out of school?'

'Well, strategic operations, obviously, but—'

'But where? For some think tank? Doing it in some dry, boring place where you'll never actually get out to see whether what you've planned is happening? You want to do it in Net Force, don't you?'

'Yeah,' Megan said. 'Of course I do. It's— I think it's one of the most important agencies we've got now, though there are probably people who would say that's overrating it.' She shifted a little uncomfortably. 'It's the cutting edge . . .'

'Well, you want to stay there, don't you? If you back off from this now, just because Winters told you to get out of danger, out of trouble— If we succeed in making it into Net Force someday, there's going to *be* danger and trouble. This is just practice. Besides – they're watching us. You *know* they're watching us. If we go in, alongside them – maybe even *ahead* of them – and crack this thing, with our eyes open and our brains hot – you think they're going to be angry about that? I don't think so. They're going to be *impressed*. If we impress them now—'

Megan nodded. 'I can't believe,' she said slowly, 'that we're not at least as good as whatever operatives they're going to send in there. Besides, we know Sarxos better than anyone they've got. That's why they asked us to go in in the first place. Because we're best . . .'

She looked up at Leif, grinned, and got up. 'I'm with you,' she said. 'Look, I'm not sure what time I'll get into the game tonight. Opting out of family night is going to take some explaining.'

'Okay . . . well, I'll go in before you, and wait for you, and I'll leave some transit in your account. We'll meet in Errint, and see if we can catch Fettick first and warn him off. The place is just a little city-state, kind of like Minsar. When you get to the city, there's a little cookshop just inside the third wall, a place called Attila's.'

Megan raised her eyebrows.

'Yeah,' Leif said, 'they make good chili there. I'll sit

there and amuse myself until you get there. Then we'll go in and engineer a chat with Fettick . . . take our time and make sure he understands.'

'All right,' Megan said. 'We do have to try. But talking someone out of a campaign is going to be interesting.'

'I think we can change his mind. After that, we can start looking around for some more indicators to what's really going on. I'm sure we can crack this if we just have a little more time . . .'

'Right. I'll see you tonight, then . . .'

She vanished.

Leif came to Errint in the late afternoon of a clearing golden day. The city stood in a small glacial valley associated with the furthest eastward-flung massif of the great northern Highpeak range. Sometime far back in the place's apparent geological history, when the continent of Sarxos was supposed to have been glaciated, a huge broad-bottomed river of ice had come grinding slowly down from the wide and snowy cirque of Mount Holdfast above the valley, and had burred the valley down into a long, gentle U-shaped trough nearly nine miles long. Now the glacier was gone, retreated to the very feet of Holdfast, with only the telltale threaded stream running down from the glacier's terminal moraine left winding down the valley, in a meander of scattered white rounded stones and the peculiar milky green-white water that betrayed a river-bed covered with glacial 'flour.'

Up on a little spur of stone which somehow had

avoided being ground down by the glacier, Errint rose. It had been a wooden city, in its earliest incarnation, but it kept burning down, and so it was finally rebuilt in stone, and its sign and sigil became the phoenix. Its population was not large, but they were famous: sturdy, independent mountain people, dangerous in battle, good with a halberd or a crossbow. They tended to keep themselves to themselves and not mix in foreign wars . . . unless the pay was good. Their city had a small but steady source of wealth from the salt and iron mines in the mountain, which they controlled jealously, telling no one the secrets of the labyrinthine ways in and out. They farmed the long, gentle, stony valley in a small way, oats and barley mostly, and tried to mind their own business.

That had become less easy of late. Argath's rise in the Northlands had meant that the kingdoms on the fringes of his realm had started looking for allies, or buffer states that would protect them from the unfriendly neighbor just over the mountain passes. To the countries to the north – meaning Argath – and to the south – meaning the realms of Duke Morgon and others – Errint looked like a perfect possibility: a small population unlikely to put up much of a fight: ground not worth much except as a buffer, so that battles fought across it wouldn't ruin its value: and the mines, source of the peerless Holdfast iron, much sought after in Sarxos for weapons.

The Errint did not take kindly to the thought of being anybody's buffer state, however. When Argath first came down out of the mountains to annex them, they had fought him and driven him back: just last year they had done it again. But then Argath had twice made the mistake of attacking into the teeth of their weather, which the Errint knew better than anyone. Even in the summer, those somnolent-looking dolomite peaks could wrap themselves around in cloud and turn ferocious: and down the valley would come screaming the killing wind, the fierce hot wind that poured itself over the northern mountain crests, stirred the few little glacial lakes to madness, and kindled thunderstorms that seemed almost pathologically fond of striking invading troops with lightning.

It was a tough nut to crack, little Errint. Not that it was uncrackable: nor was its leadership so misguided as to think so. They knew very well Argath's brooding power to the north. They had never been in a position to attack it independently. But things might be changing now . . .

So Leif stood in the open gate of the city, looking around the place, and the gate-guards, leaning on their straight sharp halberds, looked back at him with equanimity. They were big, dark-haired, blunt-featured men, typical of Errint blood, favoring leather instead of cloth for wear. Leif nodded to them, knowing that they had already sized him up as harmless and friendly – otherwise he would have been flat on the ground, with one of those oversized army can-openers stuck in his gut. The guards nodded to him, affably enough, and Leif went in.

Errint's basic structure was a little like Minsar's, except on a much smaller scale. Also, there were no outbuildings permitted beyond the fifth wall, the outermost one. The bakers and tanners and so forth were pushed well back in the rearmost curve between the fourth and fifth walls, but no one pitched tents or temporary buildings outside for the simple reason that one of those sudden summer windstorms or rainstorms could simply wash them right down off the Errint Hill and into the river. The marketplace inside the third wall, therefore, was unusually crowded with tents and awnings and tables and pallets and bales. Every day was market day in Errint: a thriving trade made its way up and down the valley's single road toward the lowlands, people who had come for metal or an animal-skin and stayed to pick up something extra, a firkin of mountain butter or the famous glacier wine.

It was late enough in the day that the market had lost much of its agitation. There were still a few cries of 'Buy my beer!' or 'Skins, good skins, here, no holes!' – but it all had a desultory feel, as if everyone was already thinking of heading out to get something to eat or drink. The one steady sound there was a ting-CLANK, ting-CLANK that Leif knew, and smiled a little as he made his way through the market stalls toward the source of it.

Here in iron-mine country, lots of people knew a little about forging – the rudiments – but a really good blacksmith was harder to find, and harder still to find was a really good farrier. They tended to travel around to where the business was good – only the very best would have a fixed place of work where they could expect clients to beat a path to their doors with their horses in tow. This one, though, was plenty good.

Leif pushed his way through the part of the market reserved for the butchers, past the last few beef carcasses hanging in the late sun with clouds of flies shrilling about them, and came to a spot by the curve of the wall where someone had parked a cart. It was from here that the rhythmic ting-CLANK sound came. Nearby, its head down and its reins fastened to an iron ring in the back end of the cart, a big, patient, blond draft horse stood. Just in front of the horse, working at an anvil lifted up onto what had been some rich Errint's mounting-stone, was a little fair man in a light, worn tan canvas shirt and well-worn leathern breeches, with a thick leather apron over it all, hammering away at a horseshoe that had just been in the portable forge-pit which had come out of his cart and now stood near the anvil on the ground. The bellows hung at hand in the cart's framework, ready to work. The farrier paused a moment to pick up the horseshoe with his tongs and shove it in among the coals to heat again. When it came up to cherry-red, he took it out with the tongs and began beating it again on the anvil.

'Wayland,' Leif said.

The face that looked up at him was deeply lined, all smile-lines. The eyes had that distant-looking expression of someone mountain-bred, though not these mountains. 'Well, it's young Leif,' Wayland said. 'Well met in the afternoon! What brings you up here this time of year?'

'Just wandering around,' Leif said, 'as usual.'

Wayland looked at him with a grin that suggested he

might be taking what Leif said with a grain of salt. 'Ah, well, may be, may be.'

'I might ask the same of you,' Leif said. 'You're not usually up here this close to autumn. I thought you'd decided you didn't want any more of this weather. Lowlands for me, I thought you said, come the fall . . .'

'Aah, it's still summer though, isn't it?' asked Wayland. He dropped his voice. 'And as for you, with your healing stone and all, I don't think you're just wandering. My money says you have some other reason to be here.'

'Hate to see you lose your bet,' said Leif, sitting down on the side-step of the cart, out of the way. For a couple of minutes he just sat and watched Wayland finish hammering the horseshoe. Wayland plunged it into a bucket of water nearby: the water boiled and hissed in a rush of steam. The horse flicked its ears back and forth, unconcerned. 'Man wants to make a living,' Wayland said casually, 'you've got to go where the business is going to be.'

'You think there's going to be business here?'

'Oh, aye,' said Wayland, fishing with the tongs in the bucket to get the horseshoe out. 'Plenty of business soon, I think.' He glanced in the direction of the city gates, up and over the walls, eastward down the long valley. 'Going to be fighting around here before long.'

He lifted the draft horse's right fore foot, caught it between his knees and turned his back on Leif for the moment. 'Who would you say?' Leif said.

For a moment Wayland didn't say anything: he glanced over his shoulder, rather hurriedly, Leif thought, and then down to his work again. Leif looked over his shoulder, the way Wayland had looked, and saw, past the various people still walking in the market-place, past the beef carcasses, a strange little shape go by. A strange small man, less than four feet high. Not, as correctness would have it, a small person, but definitely a dwarf. He was dressed in noisy, eye-hurting orange and green motley, with a scaled-down lute strung on a baldric over his shoulder.

The little man passed out of view for a moment. 'Duke Mengor has come visiting,' said Wayland, apropos of apparently nothing.

'Visiting Lord Fettick?'

'Aye, aye.' Wayland put the first of the nails into the first of the holes made for it in the horseshoe, drove the nail in halfway and then started beating what was left of it upward and outward, clenching it up and around the edge of the shoe. 'Been here a day or so, talking about whatever high lords do talk about. Nice dinner last night up at the High House—' He glanced sidewise up at the modest little castle that sat inside the city's innermost ring. 'Some talk about Fettick's daughter being of marriageable age.'

'Is she?'

Wayland's face worked, and he spat. 'Well, she's fourteen. Might be marriageable down south, but—' He raised his eyebrows. 'Well, no accounting for foreign ways . . .'

'Do you think this marriage will come off?'

'Not if something else does first,' said Wayland, very softly. 'Someone's trying to save his skin.'

127

Leif dropped his voice right down too. 'This wouldn't have anything to do with Argath, would it?'

Wayland looked at Leif sidelong, and spat into the fire: an old mountain gesture suggesting that some words were better not spoken at all, let alone too loudly. After a few seconds, 'Heard someone say that his armies were gathering,' said Wayland. 'Not sure where they are this moment, though.'

Leif nodded. 'Heard, too,' Wayland said, barely above a whisper, 'that someone who should have brought him to fight, and beaten him . . . didn't manage it.'

'Elblai,' Leif said, in a matching whisper.

'Saying is,' Wayland said, 'she got bounced.' And he spat in the fire again.

Leif thought quietly for a second, watching Wayland go back to clenching down the nails of the horseshoe. He finished the last one, then dropped the hammer and picked up a big rough file, and started rasping the edges of the nails down. 'Wayland,' Leif said, 'would have time to talk a little later?'

'Surely,' Wayland said after a moment. 'Why not?'

'Somewhere quiet.'

'You know the Scrag End down in Winetavern Street? Between the second and third walls, going sunward from the gates.'

'The place with the beehive outside it? Yeah.'

'After dark, then?'

'Fine. Two hours after sunset be all right?'

'Fine.' Wayland straightened up from his work. 'Well then, youngster—'

Leif raised a hand in casual farewell, and walked away through the market, looking idly at the few things still laid out on the stalls; bolts of cloth, a last few tired-looking cheeses.

He was glad to have run into Wayland. The man was a noticing type, worth knowing. Leif had known him for quite a while, since his first battle in Sarxos after picking up the healing-stone: they had in fact met in a field hospital, since farriers, skilled with hot metal and the cautery, were much in demand on battlefields where magic workers couldn't be found. Wayland had been surprisingly gentle with the men he had been treating, for all that the treatment itself was brutal: he missed little of the detail of what was going on around him, and had a phenomenal memory. At the moment, Leif was glad of the possibility to talk over Sarxonian matters with someone besides Megan. A variety of viewpoints never hurt.

He wandered back out in the direction of the cook-shop. And his heart jumped inside him as someone tapped his shoulder from behind.

He spun away from the tap, as his mother had taught him, and came around with his hand on his knife.

It was Megan.

She gave Leif a wry look. 'I thought you said you were going to meet me inside the cookshop.'

'Oh . . . sorry. I got distracted. I ran into somebody I knew.'

'You mean you haven't been in to pig out on the chili yet?'

His stomach abruptly growled. 'Chili,' he said.

Megan grinned. 'Come on,' she said – and then paused at the sound of a voice raised in peculiar song on the other side of the market stalls.

'What the frack is *that*?' Megan said. The voice was accompanying itself on something very like a ukulele.

> '—*Now I will sing of the doleful maid,*
> *and a doleful maid was she,*
> *Who lost her love to the merman's child*
> *In the waves of the great salt sea*—'

The owner of the voice, if you could call it that, came wandering out among the awnings and the tables, trailed by the raucous laughter and catcalls of some of the stallkeepers as the song got ruder. Its source was the dwarf in the noisy motley. He paused by one of the stalls, a fruit stall in the process of being packed up, and began strumming rather atonal chords one-handed, while trying to snatch pieces of fruit with the other. The fruitseller, a big florid woman with a wall eye, finally lost her temper and hit the dwarf over the head with an empty basket. He fell over, picked himself up again and scampered away, laughing a nasty little high-pitched laugh reminiscent of a cartoon cockroach.

Megan stared after him. 'What was *that*?' Leif said to the fruitseller.

'Gobbo,' said the fruitseller.

'Sorry?' Megan said.

'Gobbo. That's Duke Mengor's poxy little dwarf. Some kind of minstrel he is—'

'No kind of minstrel, madam, not with *that* voice,'

said one of the butcher's men who was going by with a quarter beef-carcass on his back.

'Some kind of jester, too,' said the fruitseller. 'And some kind of nuisance. Always running around, picking and thieving and looking for trouble. Getting under people's skirts—'

'You're just jealous 'cause he didn't want to get under *your* skirt, madam,' said another of the stall-keepers who was packing up.

The fruitseller rounded on the man and began to assail his ears with such a flow of language that the stallkeeper hurriedly vanished behind someone else's stall. Leif chuckled a little and turned back toward Attila's. Megan stood there a moment, gazing off toward where the dwarf had vanished.

'I don't know why,' she said to Leif, 'but he looks familiar . . .'

'Yeah . . .' Leif looked where she did, and then said, 'I'll tell you why. You saw him in Minsar.'

'I did? Maybe I did.' Then she remembered the strange little figure with the sword, running through the torchlit marketplace, laughing that bizarre small laugh. She shuddered – she couldn't quite figure out why. 'If he was all the way over there,' she said softly, 'what's he doing all the way over *here* of a sudden?'

Leif took her arm and tugged her toward Attila's. 'Look,' he said, '*we* were all the way over there, and now we're all the way over *here*. Nothing odd about it.'

'You sure?' Megan said.

She watched Leif get that thinking look . . . and

slowly the look began to shift into something else: suspicion.

'I wonder,' he said.

'So do I. But first things first,' Megan said, and this time it was she who took Leif's arm. 'It's tough to wonder on an empty stomach.'

'All right,' he said. 'And then . . . afterwards . . . we have a meeting.'

'Oh?'

'Come on . . . I'll tell you all about it. Assuming I can talk at all while we're eating. This chili is *so hot* . . .'

'How hot is it?'

'They use it to discipline dragons . . .'

'Come on. I'm ready . . .!'

About an hour later, they were both sitting alone in a corner at Attila's, trying to recover from their dinner. 'I can't believe I ate that,' Megan said. 'I can't believe I ate that *twice*.' She was looking at the remains of her second bowl.

Leif chuckled and had a swig of his drink. There was no cure for Attila's chili except cold sweet tea with cream, so both of them were drinking that, out of tall ceramic cups. 'I feel sorry for the dragons you were mentioning,' Megan said.

Leif cocked an eye at the window. 'It's getting close to sunset,' Leif said. 'We should probably go ahead.'

'Okay. But finish telling me what you started to,' Megan said, 'about Wayland.'

'Oh, no, I was finished.'

'It was something about his name.'

'Oh, that . . . it's just a generic name for a wandering smith. A small joke. But he's a good one. And he gets around. He hears a lot. There was something else I was going to mention before we went to see him, though.'

Leif glanced around them. The lady who owned Attila's had gone out to stand in the cool of the approaching evening, leaning against the door opening into the marketplace plaza, where she was chatting with some passer-by.

Leif said quietly, 'Before I came into Sarxos today, I wanted to do some work on something else that occurred to me.'

'Oh?'

'Well, you said that there had to be some more systematic way to go about this search for the bouncer. It seemed to me that you were right. So I thought, if it's not a question of who's beating Argath in battle – because plainly we're meant to think that it is – then the question becomes who, what player or character, has *also* been beaten in battles or skirmishes by the same people? By *all* the same people who've beaten Argath?'

Megan looked at him thoughtfully. 'See,' Leif said, 'you have to consider the problem as if it were a problem in set theory, something you could set up as a Venn diagram, something that looks sort of like a Sarxos version of a Mastercard logo. You have to look at the whole history of battle in Sarxos for a couple of years, to see where there are overlaps in terms of who was fighting whom. And the overlaps have to be *exact*, for the cover to be successful. Do you follow me?'

Megan blinked and then nodded. She knew analysis was one of Leif's strong points; it was just slightly startling to see him pull it out of the hat like this. 'Okay,' she said. 'So what did you find?'

'Well, to begin with, the business of having battles in Sarxos isn't terribly organized. It's not like there's a set schedule or anything. But there *is* a tendency for members of a given group of players to fight most of the other members of the same group – the groupings being loosely based on area. Partly it's just the logistics of the game. It's costly in terms of weeks of game-time to move large numbers of people, large armies, from one end of Sarxos to the other: it's just not logistically feasible. When's the last time you heard of a North-continent-against-South-continent battle?'

Megan shook her head. 'I don't think I ever have.'

'There *was* one,' Leif said, 'but it was twelve years ago, game-time, and it bankrupted both sides. Worse, no one even actually *won* it – it came out a stalemate, because several countries on the borders of both the North-continent and South-continent realms that were fighting took that opportunity to attack the countries that were attacking each other. It was a situation kind of like the one during the American Revolution, but much worse: the way France and the Netherlands and other countries, diplomatically or in the field, took the opportunity to gang up on Britain while Britain was trying to have a war with the United States.

'But, anyway, 'tween-continent wars just don't seem to happen here any more: there's no percentage in it.' Leif leaned back in his seat. 'So you'll get countries who can raise enough people for armies – which is most of them; everyone loves to fight, and half the people in Sarxos are here for "battlefield work" – and who, over the course of the late spring-summer-early autumn campaign season, tend to fight everyone else available during that period. They end up going to war with practically everyone in that "league" or "group," simply because they're physically close. The "leagues" are pretty evenly spread across the total play area.'

'Isn't that a little weird?'

'In the real world, maybe it is. But here— I sat down with the map of Sarxos, and I noticed something very interesting about what Rodrigues did when he was building this place. He made sure there are *no* populated areas completely lacking in strategic value. No matter where you live, no matter what country you've inherited or conquered, there's always something useful about it. But more to the point, there's always somewhere *more* interesting, someplace with things you could use, just over the horizon or the hill. You'll have one rich country sandwiched between two or three smaller, poorer ones. Or a big, powerful country will find itself surrounded by a number of other countries that just aren't feasible for it to attack. Look at Errint, for example. Argath is just over that way, and he should have found it easy to overrun this place with his big armies, but he can't because of the mountain range between him and Errint. Its passes were apparently very carefully placed to make invasion difficult.'

'Built-in frustration,' Megan said.

'More than just that, I think,' Leif said. 'Rod in his

infinite wisdom—' Leif glanced at the ceiling with an amused look – 'has built the seeds of conflict into this place. But also the seeds of stability, to keep everything balanced. He's been very subtle about it.'

'Did you figure all this out yourself?' Megan said, both impressed and amused.

'Huh? Most of it,' Leif said. 'A couple of books have been written on Sarxos, but by and large the authors didn't know what they were talking about, or they got caught up in the wonder of the external details, the computer interface and the points system and all, and never got into any depth.'

'Well, it all sounds like good sense to me,' Megan said. 'If you're a game designer, you want to make sure your players don't get bored. Though I'll say that Sarxos doesn't seem to be in any danger of that.'

'True enough. But Rod has been sneaky about it. Leaving Arstan and Lidios out of the equation – they're special cases because of the 'gunpowder rule,' and mostly they fight each other rather than other countries – it seems to me as if there are two alternating sets of pressures in the game. One is brought to bear by the players. They want to keep things working the way they're working, by and large, and they only want things to change in ways that suit them. The other set of pressures, I think, comes from Rod: pressures to make sure that situations that are static don't stay static forever, and to keep things which are changing from changing too quickly, or too much. If you look at the abstracts of play for the last ten game-years, you get a sense that here and there, Sarxos is being given a nudge . . . a kick. A trend will start going in one direction in one country – remember that slavery thing in Dorlien? – and then something will happen to sort of nudge the place back on course. Or another place will have behaved the same way for a long time, and something will happen, all of a sudden, seemingly just at the right moment to push it off the tracks and off in a completely new direction.'

Megan paused for a moment. 'It sounds like a great way to keep things going. But you're not suggesting,' she said, her face changing suddenly, 'that these bounces – are *themselves* some kind of "nudge"? You don't think that Rodrigues – that *Rod*—'

Leif looked at her, nodding slowly. 'I was wondering,' he said, 'if that conclusion would be one you would reach too.'

Megan sat and thought. 'You know,' she said, 'paranoia is a terrible thing. It starts creeping in everywhere . . .'

'Yeah,' Leif said. 'But the question remains: *is* this just paranoia, or not? If the Argath connection is actually a cover for something, for someone's revenge for some grudge, or something else more obscure, then, from the way things look to me, they first sat down and did a most careful analysis on the game – on the structure of the game and the way it's set up to run – looking to see where they could most effectively interfere, and how they could interfere so that it could best be blamed on somebody else. If you're saying that one person in a good position to do that would be the game designer himself, the one who runs the place—'

Megan shook her head, troubled. 'A lot of other people would be in that position, too.'

'Yeah, I know. But it's a possibility we've got to consider.'

Megan started turning her tea cup around and around. 'A gamesmaster can run his game however he likes . . . but why would he start bouncing his paying customers? Without motivation, the theory won't hold water.'

'It's not a theory yet. Just a possibility.'

'Sherlock Holmes wouldn't dignify it with even that term, I don't think.' But the Megan shrugged. There was no point in running this into the ground right now. 'So let's get less specific. You sound pretty sure now that someone else besides Argath is responsible for the bounces. You think that it's somebody who has been defeated by all the same people that Argath has been defeated by. Fine. How many people is that?'

'Six,' Leif said. 'Generals or commanders named Hunsal, Orieta, Walse, Rutin, Lateran, and Balk the Screw.'

'What a name,' Megan said.

'Yeah. Well, when you analyze the data this way, you get a little help, because all these players are "based" in the northeastern North-continent area. Either their cities, realms or armies are there, or the battles took place in that "league area." '

'Sounds like this analysis increases the chances of the real bouncer being one of those six people. If not Argath.'

'That's right. At least, that's how it looks to me. Can

you think of any other way to read it?'

Megan shook her head. 'Not instantly. I'd still want to look at the hard data for myself . . . but it would be second-guessing. This is your specialty, and if this is the way you see it, I'm willing to buy in.'

'Great. So that would seem to be our next line of investigation, then,' Leif said. 'Oh – you *did* get your report ready for Winters, didn't you?'

'Yeah. He should be getting it— Wait a minute. Game intervention,' Megan said to the air.

'Waiting.'

'Time check, home base.'

'Nine-forty-three PM.'

'Finished. Fifteen minutes ago,' Megan said. 'And how about you?'

'Oh, yeah, mine's on timed release – he'll have it in an hour or so.'

'And *this* line of investigation?' Megan said, looking at him with a sly expression. 'Did you tell him about this new information you've dug up?'

'Um, well . . .'

'We're holding out on him to see what we can do first, huh?' Megan said.

'Well, that seems consonant with what we discussed earlier . . . doesn't it?'

Megan felt just slightly inclined to squirm. At the same time, she also felt that they might really be onto something here. 'Look, let's just run with this for a day or two more,' Leif said. 'We're so close, I know it. And with no new battles really imminent—'

'I agree with you about following up on this for

another day or so,' Megan said, 'but not on the false premise that there are no battles coming right away. We can't assume that those are going to have anything to do with our bouncer attacking anyone or refraining from attacking them. I think he's going to bounce anybody he likes now, whenever he's good and ready, and I'd like to do as much work on this as I can tonight. After we talk to Wayland, we should get right in touch with Fettick, and then our next time in here, with Duchess Morn. We've got to make sure they're warned, and that they believe the warning.'

'Yeah. Then we need to start talking to those six generals,' said Leif, 'or talking to people about them. It's going to use a lot of transit, but—' he shrugged.

'Yeah, well, you can split some of the footwork with me,' Megan said. 'I've got some transit – not as much as you have, maybe, but this is important. But we need to get our butts in gear. It may take time to gather enough information about these six to find out which of them is the most likely to be the bouncer.'

'And then what do we do? If we're sure we've found the right person, that is?'

'Call Net Force,' Megan said. 'Hand them everything we've got, and tell them to go get that bouncer.'

'I would very much want to insist on being in at the "kill," ' Leif said.

' "Insist"? To whom? Winters?' Megan gave him a skeptical look. 'You want an estimate of your chances at getting away with that?'

'Uh. Well . . . I'd real strongly suggest it, anyway. Just for satisfaction's sake.'

'It would be nice to be there, or here, when it happens,' Megan said. 'I wouldn't count on it, myself. I think the "grownups" may want us safely out of the way. But satisfaction? There'll be plenty of that when they throw the bouncer in the can.' The image of Elblai's face as she was taken into the hospital, her violet eyes closed, her face covered with violet bruising, was very much with Megan. 'And either way, we'll get the glory. Net Force'll know who did the legwork.'

'Fair enough. Come on,' Leif said, and got up, stretching. 'Let's get out of here.'

They took a last swig of their beer, then headed out into the street themselves, and started walking slowly back toward the marketplace. 'Pity we couldn't take care of this tonight,' Megan said.

Leif shrugged. 'Never mind. Are you going to be able to log in tomorrow morning early? That's when we'll need to take care of this.'

'Shouldn't be any problem. Mornings are quiet around my place. It's evenings that're the—'

She suddenly fell silent.

'Huh?' Leif said.

'It's nothing,' she said in a low voice. 'Just keep walking.'

'It's *not* nothing. *What is it?*'

'It's evenings that're the problem,' Megan went on, looking sideways down an alley as they passed it. 'My father can be an incredible nuisance about family nights. *It's him again,*' she whispered.

'Oh, well, *fathers,*' Leif said as they walked. Megan

saw that he too was trying to look down the alley she had been looking down, without seeming to do so. But he still looked baffled. *I guess my night vision must be better than his* . . . 'They're pains, but you can't live without them, and you can't shoot them . . . *Him, who?*'

'*Gobbo*,' she whispered. 'Once might be a coincidence . . . twice might be an accident . . . but three times is enemy action.'

'Sorry?'

'He's following us.'

'Are you sure?'

'He has to be. And you know what? He's been following us since Minsar.'

'It could be paranoia, Megan . . .'

'It's not.' She turned suddenly into another alleyway, and pulled Leif in after her. For a moment they both leaned against one of the damp stone walls in the dead silence.

Not quite dead. A scurry of feet, then nothing. Then another scurry, closer.

'Down there,' Leif whispered.

'Maybe he is. I'm not waiting. I don't like being followed . . . it makes me want to practice dwarf-chucking.'

'What?'

'Dwarf-chucking. A very old and very incorrect sport. My mother would be shocked to even hear me mention it.' Megan grinned, looked around them. 'Where are we?'

'Between the third and fourth walls.'

'No, I mean which way is east?'

Well ahead of them, leftward against one stone wall, was a patch of moonlight. Leif pointed off to the right.

'Oh, yeah,' Megan said softly, and thought for a moment. Being an incurable map-reader, Megan had had a good look at the game's stored map of Errint before coming in today. Now she compared the spot where they stood with her memory of the map, and considered for another second or so.

'All right,' she whispered then. 'There's a gate in the wall to your left about sixty yards ahead. It goes through into the next circle. I'm going to leave you. Count thirty seconds and then follow me. Walk down the middle of the street. Don't stop at the gate: just keep going.'

'What are you going to do?'

She smiled. And she vanished.

Leif stared. She had *not* used game-based magic – there was a typical aura, a feel in the air, associated with magic use at close range, which he would have detected. But very quietly, very simply between one blink and one breath and the next, Megan had stopped being where he had thought she should have been. It was a little unnerving.

One, two, three, he thought, wondering as always whether his seconds were as accurate as he thought they were. Leif listened to the sleeping city, listened hard. Somewhere, up high, a bat made its tiny *squee-squee-squee* of sonar, possibly targeting bugs attracted to the lights still burning in the windows of the towers of the High House. Nothing else moved.

Scuffle . . . scurry

Fifteen, sixteen, seventeen, eighteen, Leif thought. *Nineteen, twenty . . .*

Out in the open country, there was a brief, distant, astonishing burst of sweet-voiced song. A nightingale. It ran its descant through to its end, almost making Leif forget where he was in his counting. For a moment, the scurrying stopped. Then it started again.

—twenty-eight, twenty-nine, thirty—

Leif stepped out into the street and began walking calmly down toward the gate. He was not particularly calm. Errint was a city where it was permissible to carry weapons within the walls, so he had a knife. He was good enough with it to make serious trouble for anyone who tried anything, and he had enough general self-defense training to make him feel comfortable in any large real-world city. But this was *not* any large real-world city. This was Sarxos, and you never knew when someone was going to jump at you out of a dark alley carrying a loaded cockatrice . . . against which front snap-kicks would do you no good at all.

Leif walked on, resisting the temptation to whistle. It might make you feel better in the dark, but it also pinpointed your location for someone whose night vision might be no better than his. He strolled, as calmly as he could, and passed the square of moonlight on the left-hand wall, just a thin ray of it passing between two taller buildings on the east side. The gate Megan had mentioned was maybe another twenty yards on. Very, very quietly, Leif reached down and started loosening his knife in its sheath.

Behind him, very softly, something went *scuffle*.

He didn't stop to look behind, though he was sorely tempted. Leif kept walking. His mother's voice said in his head, *No common thug ever sneaks up* right *behind you. They always break into a run, those last few steps. If it's a professional stalking you, you don't have a hope. You're probably dead already. But if it's just a thug, so long as you can't hear those last few steps, you've still got at least a few feet between you and him or her. When you hear those steps, though, they're in reaching range. Do something quick—*

Leif just went strolling on.

Scurry. Scuffle – pause – *scurry*, pause—

He kept walking.

There was the gate, a faint, wide, arched dimness in the darkness of the left-hand wall. Leif walked innocently past it, not turning his head to look through it, just taking his time, though he could see by peripheral vision that no one was there.

Scuffle.

Footsteps. Soft shoes on the stones. Much closer now.

Leif swallowed.

Scurry, scuffle—

—and someone breaking into a run—

Leif whirled, whipping the knife out, going forward just enough on the balls of his feet to jump or run.

He never had a chance to do either. A dark shape shot out of the gateway and got jumbled up with the very small dark blot that had been running at him. Leif was uncertain what happened next, except that the two dark forms seemed to consolidate . . . and then one of them flew away from the other, and into the wall opposite the gate, with stunning force. There was a shriek, cut off suddenly as the smaller form slid down the wall and hit the cobblestones.

Leif hurried over. Megan was standing there, not even looking particularly winded. She was standing over that smaller shape, now, her hands on her hips, looking down with an expression that was hard to make out in the darkness, but it looked thoughtful.

'He weighs nearly as much as my number-three brother,' she said mildly. 'Interesting. All right, Gobbo, get up off your butt, it wasn't that bad.'

The dwarf lay moaning and sniveling on the ground. 'Don't hurt me, don't do that again!'

Megan reached down and hoisted Gobbo up by the front of his motley, and briefly held him straight-armed against the wall at nearly eye level. She and Leif studied his face. It was that of a middle-aged man, much collapsed together because of his dwarfism: a nasty face, eloquent of much troublemaking.

'I'm a very important person, I can get you in a lot of trouble!' the dwarf squealed. 'Let me go!'

'Oh, yeah,' Leif said, 'we're shaking, the two of us. Was that dwarf-chucking?' he said to Megan.

'Very incorrect,' she said, in an abstracted tone of voice. 'But you could get used to it.'

The dwarf's face spasmed with fear. 'Don't!'

'Why were you following us?' Leif said.

'And why have you been following us since Minsar?'

said Megan. 'Answers, quick – or I'll chuck you right over this wall, honest, and we'll see how important *gravity* thinks you are when you come down.'

'What makes you think—'

Megan lifted him a little higher.

'Your arm getting tired?' Leif said. 'I could take him. I can press almost one-fifty these days.'

'No,' Megan said, 'no need. I won't wait much longer. Gobbo, this is your last chance. I saw a lady get hurt today, and it's put me in a real bad mood, and made me short-tempered with people who don't answer reasonable questions.' She started to lift him higher.

The dwarf looked at her, a strange expression. 'Put me down,' he said, 'and I'll tell you what you want to know.'

Megan looked at him for a moment, then put him down.

'All right,' she said. 'Let's hear it.'

The dwarf began feeling around in his pockets. Megan was watching him like a hawk. Leif was wondering what those pockets might conceal—

'Here,' the dwarf said, and reached up, holding out something for Megan to take.

She reached down her hand and took it, curious. She lifted it close to her eyes, turned it over and over in the dimness. It looked like a coin, except that its edges were smooth, not milled. It was not made of metal, either. It was a circle of some dark mineral, with a design engraved on it. Megan held it upward toward another of the squares of moonlight high up on a nearby wall, and looked at it, through it. So did Leif. He caught a wink of the darkest red, even in this silver light. The thing was made of pigeon's blood ruby, and deeply engraved in it, in an old uncial font, was the letter *S*.

Megan looked at Leif with an expression on her face. 'Game intervention,' she said.

'Listening.'

'Identify this object.'

'Object is identified as the Creator's Token,' said the computer voice. 'The Sigil of Sarxos – positive in-game identification of the game designer and copyright holder.'

Both of them looked down at the dwarf in complete astonishment.

'Yes,' Gobbo said, in an entirely different voice. 'I'm Chris Rodrigues.'

Chapter Four

They finally wound up at Attila's again. It was empty
when they got there, except for a young man who took
care of the door.

The slit in the door came open. 'Show him what I
gave you,' said 'Gobbo.'

Megan held up the ruby token for the doorman to
see. His eyes, seen through the slit, widened: the slit
closed, and the door opened for them.

Inside, as they went in, the young man was looking
with utter astonishment at Megan. 'You?'

'No, no, *him*,' she said, indicating the dwarf. Except
that he wasn't a dwarf any more.

Suddenly a tallish guy was standing there, in jeans
and a T-shirt and somewhat beat-up-looking sneakers:
a big-boned man, somewhere in his early middle years,
with curly unruly hair and a curly beard, and brown
eyes, the kindliest eyes Megan thought she had ever
seen. 'Listen,' said, Rodrigues, 'I know you'd love to
talk to me, but I need to talk to these people just now,
and it's urgent. Can I come back and see you next
week – would that be OK?'

149

'Uh, yeah, sure, fine,' said the young man. 'You'll make sure you shut the door when you go out—'

'No problem.'

The doorkeeper went out the front door, closed it behind him.

Chris stood there for a moment, then picked up the bolt and dropped it in place, and came back to sit at the rearmost table.

Leif, sitting there staring at Rodrigues, was still having trouble coping with it all. 'It's really *you*, isn't it?'

'Of course it is. There's no faking this.' Chris gave the token on the table a little push. 'I always anticipated that sometimes I would need to make my presence known: so I made sure there was a way for players to know it was me, one that couldn't be faked.'

Megan nodded. 'Why *were* you following us?' she said.

'Because you're something to do with these bounces, aren't you?'

She and Leif stared at Rodrigues in complete shock. 'No, I don't mean that you're involved with them! But you've been hanging around with some people who may have been involved . . . haven't you? And one of them – Ellen. Elblai—'

'Yes. We were with her just last night.'

'So I saw from the game-logs. And the descriptions of you that her niece gave me were quite precise.' Rodrigues sat back. 'So I thought I would have a look at you myself – this was before Elblai, mind you – and then followed you here: I had the system alert me when you came back into gameplay.'

'I have to tell you,' said Leif, 'we're not just doing this for fun. We're with the Explorers . . . we're with Net Force.'

'Net Force, yeah,' Rodrigues said, and leaned forward on the table, running his hands through his hair. 'Yeah, I've had some people from there in here already today. Naturally the Elblai situation brought them in, and I'm glad they came. But I don't know what they can do. I'm not sure what any of us can do . . .'

He sounded despondent. Megan said, 'Whoever has been doing this . . . they can't be doing it tracelessly. And they have been leaving some clues behind . . . we think. It's only a matter of time before we, or the senior Net Force operatives, work out—'

Rodrigues looked up. 'Time,' he said. 'How much of that do we have before this person bounces someone else? And does it violently? The early bounces, the smash-and-ruin bounces, those were bad enough. This is not the kind of thing I wanted happening in my game.'

'We know,' Leif said. 'We didn't think so either. So we came in and started looking around to see what we could find out . . .'

'The same here,' said Rodrigues. 'But I didn't expect to get flung at a wall.'

'Sorry,' Megan said, blushing hot. 'I thought you were—'

'Some little creep dwarf,' said Rodrigues, grinning. 'Yes. He's a favorite of mine, Gobbo.'

'Is he the character you run, then?' said Leif.

'One of about twenty,' Rodrigues said. 'Some of them are fairly quiet . . . some of them are pretty outrageous. They give me a chance to wander around and interact with people in different ways . . . and make sure they're playing the Game correctly.' He smiled a little. 'One of the pleasures of playing God. Or Rod.' The smile got more ironic.

'But the past few months, I've been doing it more with an eye to seeing what I can find out about these bounces. It's not just that I don't like my creation being used this way . . . which I don't. But Sarxos has always had a reputation as a safe place, a place where the game was played fairly . . . not one of those fly-by-night operations where the gamesmaster changes the rules on you without warning. And it's not just a game, of course: it's a consumer-driven operation. You have to treat your customers right. If word gets out that this kind of thing is starting to happen – if there's even one more instance of an attack like the one on Elblai – it's going to do immense damage to the game. It could be shut down. I leave to your imagination the kind of legal trouble that could ensue. The bottom-line boys at the parent company would *not* be happy with me, not at all.'

Leif was studying the table with a rather noncommittal look on his face. 'Look,' Rodrigues said, just a little sharply, 'I'm already a millionaire so many times over that it's not even fun counting it at night any more when I need to fall asleep. I have a great privilege: I get to do what I love to make my living. There's nothing better than that. But there are more important things than my pleasure, and a whole lot more important than money. If there's no other way to stop this, I'll damn well see the game shut down. A lot of people disappointed is better than a few people dead. And that's where it's heading, if you ask me. I wish to God I was wrong, but I'm a pessimist at heart – that's why I'm such a good designer.'

He sighed. 'Anyhow, I've told the Net Force people that I'll cooperate with them every way I can. The company won't let me give them the game-logs directly, they're moaning about proprietary information, but I can read them and pass excerpted information on. They were asking about yours, by the way.'

Megan nodded. 'We know. There's e-mail going out shortly – if it hasn't already gone – giving my release.'

'Okay, that's fine. You too?' He looked at Leif.

'Yeah.'

'Good.'

'What about *your* game-logs?' Leif said suddenly.

Rodrigues looked at him. Megan briefly felt as if she wished the Earth would open and swallow her.

'How do you mean?'

'The Net Force people may suggest to you,' Leif said in a very even and almost gentle voice, 'that one possibility is that you might have been involved with these bounces.'

'Now why would I do a thing like that?' Rodrigues said, looking at Leif strangely.

'I have no idea,' Leif said, 'and I don't believe it myself. But—' He shrugged.

153

'Well,' said Rodrigues, 'as for that, the game-servers keep track of me exactly the way they do of everyone else. You can never tell, I might go crazy and try to sabotage the code.' He made that ironic 'fat-chance' expression which seemed to appear on his face about once every couple of minutes. 'The server logs will confirm when I was in here . . . which frankly is most of my waking hours: if I'm not doing maintenance on bugs, which contrary to popular belief pop up constantly, then I'm in the game itself, walking up and down to see who's naughty and who's nice. There's fortunately no way to forge that information.'

Megan looked at Leif, and Leif looked back. 'You know,' Megan said, 'we were talking about a more structured way to conduct our search—' She took a few moments to explain to him the roundabout train of logic they had been following. 'But there's a possibility here,' she said. 'The logs—'

Leif looked at her. 'The server logs,' Megan said. 'They keep track of everybody who's playing, everybody who's in the game. But also – by process of elimination – they'll show you when everyone who's a player is *not* in the game. And the bounces – the physical attacks on equipment, and in Elblai's case, on people – happened when the player committing the attacks was physically *not* in the game. If we could run a search through the computers—'

Rodrigues looked at her a little sadly. 'Do you know,' he said, 'how many hundreds of thousands, sometimes millions, of people, might be out of the game at any given moment? You're going to have to find some other criterion to sort by, and cut down the size of that sample.'

'We've got several other sets of criteria,' Leif said. 'In fact, we've got one six-name list I'd really like to run against the server logs.'

'Which six names?'

'Orieta, Hunsal, Balk the Screw . . .'

Rodrigues shook his head. 'Where do they get some of these names . . .'

'. . . Rutin, Walse, and Lateran.'

'Huh,' Rodrigues said. 'All generals and war-leaders, huh? How did you get interested in these particular names?'

Leif told him.

'Well,' Rodrigues said, 'those six we certainly should be able to check . . .'

'Do you have all the times of the actual attacks?' Megan said.

'Oh, yes, believe me.' Rodrigues laced his fingers together, leaned his chin on them. 'Game intervention.'

'Listening.'

'This is the boss.'

'Verified.'

'Access the real-world timings of attacks on bounced players.'

'Accessed. Holding in store.'

'Access server records for game usage for the following players: Hunsal, Rutin, Orieta, Walse, Balk the Screw, and Lateran.'

'Accessed. Holding in store.'

'Compare.'

155

'Comparing. Criteria?'

'Identify which players were outside the game at the times of the attacks.'

Leif and Megan held very still.

'Walse, outside at attack one, attack three. Orieta, outside at attack five. Balk the Screw, outside at attack seven. All other players were in-game at all times of attack.'

Megan and Leif looked at each other. Megan mouthed silently, *Not useful* . . .

Leif made a face. 'All the others were playing . . .'

'So the computer says.'

'What are the chances it could be wrong?' said Leif. 'Or that its programming or its logs could have been tampered with?'

Rodrigues laughed softly. 'It's a nice try,' he said, 'but you have no idea how stringently controlled our system is, or how ruthlessly access to it is managed. The computer itself writes code: we have no human programmers handling that any more – the machine's plenty heuristic enough to handle it, and besides, there's umpty billion lines of code to deal with. No number of humans, monkeys or other primates chained to keyboards could possibly work fast enough to meet the system's needs. I just tell the machinery what's needed, and it does it. No one else has access to code, or to the server logs, except a couple of people at the parent company. And there's no way they'd be involved with this . . . they handle the logs only for archival purposes. Everything's encrypted anyway, the same as the private-play keys and so forth.'

'So there's no way that those could be tampered with . . .'

'No. Believe me,' Rodrigues said, 'we have a lot of interest from other parties who've used Sarxos, its code and its basic structure, as a testbed for other kinds of simulations, ones which aren't public. We keep our operation tight as a drum because of those affiliations.'

'But those three who were out during the attacks,' Megan said. 'There's no telling where they were, then—'

'Well, there is, to a certain extent,' Rodrigues said, 'because you can check the logs and see how soon they came back in again. Game intervention.'

'Listening.'

'Look at excerpted logs. Note if any of these players was absent from play for more than . . . one hour.'

'Walse. Absent for four hours thirteen minutes.'

'And returned to gameplay again.'

'Yes.'

'There's only one problem,' said Rodrigues, getting a slightly unfocused look which suggested to Megan that he was looking at some kind of display in the air that he could see and they couldn't. 'The first attack was in Austin, Texas, and Walse lives in Ulan Bator. Even a nearspace transport isn't going to be able to get you from Outer Mongolia to Texas in four hours. For one thing, there're no direct flights. Think how many times you'd have to change . . .' He shook his head. 'No, that won't work . . .'

He sat back, folded his arms. 'It's possible,' he said,

'that the line of reasoning you're following isn't really a valid one.'

'It's all we've got,' said Megan.

'Listen, I'm not trying to put you down,' said Rodrigues. 'I haven't got anything better. I've tried processing this data every way I could, and I'm stumped. I'm really hoping that your Net Force people can do something for me now, because I'm at my wits' end. I'll tell you, though – when we catch whoever this is—'

'When,' Megan said, and smiled a little. She liked the sound of certainty . . . but all the same it made her sad. She kept thinking of Elblai.

'Have you heard anything about Elblai – Ellen?' she said.

'She's out of surgery,' Rodrigues said, 'but she's still not conscious. She's on my mind . . .' He sighed. 'Listen, though. I have to thank you two for wanting to help, for trying to make a difference . . . Is there anything I can do for you?'

Megan shook her head. 'Not at the moment.'

Leif said suddenly, 'We could use some extra transit allowance. I've blown a lot of mine on this.'

Rodrigues chuckled. 'You're going to keep working on this problem?'

They nodded.

'Uh, consider your accounts open-ended until this is sorted out. Game intervention—'

'Listening.'

'This is the boss. See to it that characters Brown Meg and Leif Hedgewizard have open accounts from this time stamp until further notice from me.'

'Done.'

'One less thing for you to worry about, anyway.'

He sighed, looking down at his folded hands on the table, then looked up again. 'I love this place,' he said. 'You should have seen it when it started. Little scratchy, sketchy, video-only universe: you could have fitted the whole thing into a PC.' He laughed. 'Then it got out of hand. They do that, supposedly, worlds: get out of the control of their creators. Now I've got something like four million users . . . people inhabiting a world. People who really seem to think it's special.' More soft laughter. 'I got an e-mail from somebody a few months ago saying that we should petition the government to get them to let us terraform Mars, and set up Sarxos there. I get a lot of mail from people who'd like to move. I mean, this—' he thumped the table gently. 'This is pretty real, pretty good. You can eat here, drink here, sleep here, fight here . . . do all kinds of things here. But you can't *stay*. People have started saying that they want to stay here . . . live here.'

He shook his head. 'The only thing I didn't foresee . . . is that people would start doing things to each other in the real world based on what they do or don't do here. This has never been a peaceful place. It wasn't built to be a peaceful place. It's a war game! Though peace keeps breaking out . . . and that always surprised me, that people wanted to live here, not just campaign all over the countryside and fight each other to a standstill. But now . . . it's like the serpent has gotten into Eden. I don't like this serpent. I want to stomp its ugly head.'

'So do we,' said Megan.

'I know. That's why we're having this conversation.'

'We intend,' Leif said, 'to keep going . . . until we find the serpent. And stomp it.'

'Do,' Rodrigues said. 'This kind of abuse, if it once takes root and it's not dealt with immediately . . . it's going to tear this world apart. I don't want to see that.' He looked around him at the splintery walls, and the shambolic-looking roof, and the cobblestones and the stuff spilled on them. 'I don't want all this to vanish. This, and the mountain ranges where the basilisks nest, and the oceans with the sea monsters in them, and the moonlight . . . the stars . . . the people who come to my world to play . . . I don't want to see it all collapsed and put away in a box. I want it to outlive me. That would be a good immortality, to have a world that kept going while its maker was gone, or in hiding . . .' He smiled a little. 'Sort of like what we have now, out there in the physical world.'

Rodrigues looked at them, intense. 'Do what you can . . . but be careful. If you're going to do this, I can't be responsible . . . you signed the waiver when you came in.'

'We're pretty good at responsible,' Megan said. 'We'll manage.'

'Okay. Here, take this.' He reached into his pocket, came out with another token with the *S* on it: not ruby, this one, but plain gold, or at least it looked like it. 'You're going to be working together, so just take this one then. If you need something from the system – information about other players, within reason, or extra abilities – you're a wizard, you know the kind of things I mean – query the system. It'll give them to you. This also com-links to me or my account. You can leave me e-mail, or talk to me if I'm in the game.'

'Hey, thanks. This is really—'

'Don't thank me. I should be thanking you for what you're doing. There are a few others like you who're making discreet inquiries. I figure the more of us who're looking, the better it is. But in the meantime, just *be careful*.'

'We will,' Leif said.

Rodrigues stood up. 'Okay . . . it's getting late at home where I am. I've gotta go. Thanks again.'

They nodded to him. Rodrigues sketched a little wave at them . . . then, with a pop of displaced air, vanished.

Leif and Megan looked at each other. 'Not one of the six,' Leif said. '*Merde*.'

'Back to the drawing board . . .' said Megan.

They got up and left the Scrag End, carefully closing the door behind them.

Wayland was waiting for them in the marketplace in the morning, all packed up and ready to go. He had on what Leif remembered as his 'travelling hat,' a large floppy one with a bedraggled feather that made him look like a cross between a run-down Musketeer and an unemployed Norse god. 'I haven't been up to the High House yet today,' he said, leading them up into the next circle of the city, 'but there shouldn't be any trouble with finding old Tald the major-domo. He'll get you in to see the Lord right enough. Fettick isn't as standoffish as some of them are, anyway. No big ceremonies up in these parts. People wouldn't stand for it . . .'

'I thought they liked ceremonies up here,' Leif said. 'There's the Winterfest, after all, when they burn the straw man, and the Spring Madness when everybody has to get drunk for three days . . .'

'Probably old Tald wouldn't care for that,' Wayland said, going through the gate leading up into the next circle, and waving at some acquaintance up the road as they went along. 'But he's all right, he won't give you trouble.'

Megan glanced at Wayland, a little lost by the sudden obliquity. But he was turned through another gate ahead of them, with Leif behind him. She shrugged and went on after them.

The innermost wall of Errint was the old castle itself, built of glacier-boulders which had been sliced neatly into blocks as if they had been so much cheese. 'How the Old People did that, we still don't know,' Wayland said, looking up at the walls. 'No kind of magic you can get these days.'

'Might've been lasers,' Megan said, looking at the smoothness of the cuts, and the way the surfaces were glazed without being polished. Inside she was thinking with some admiration of the creativity of a man who could take the time to leave details like this all over his world: not just elaborate or unusual workmanship, but mysteries and puzzles to work over at any of several levels – the place itself could be the subject of hours of cheerful pastime as you tried to work out whether Rod had just tossed in some detail as a throwaway, or meant you to mull it over and find some hidden meaning therein. And there was always the possible joke that there *was* no meaning: the kind of joke that Megan suspected a Creator might be inclined to pull.

'It's pretty enough, that's for sure,' Wayland said, and led them up to the gates of the castle, which were open. Out in its front courtyard, people were spreading out laundry to dry in the sun, and a big florid man in dark blue was walking around and visibly bossing everybody, waving his hands, giving directions. As the three of them walked in, he immediately boomed at Wayland, 'No vacancies, good smith, there are no further employment opportunities here—!'

'Master Tald,' Wayland said, 'don't you start shouting, these people are here on business!'

'What kind of business?'

'Better ask them,' Wayland said.

Leif bowed politely enough to the major-domo and said, 'Sir, if possible we need to see Lord Fettick, on a matter of some urgency.'

'Now, I don't know about that, young man, he's very busy today—'

'You think it was magic they used on these stones?' Megan said suddenly to Wayland, pointing up at the closest wall. Wayland turned to follow the gesture, and as she did so, Leif slipped the token out of his pocket and showed it briefly to Tald.

Tald's eyes got wide. 'Well,' he said, 'it's early yet, and I doubt the newest appointments will be along for some time. Come on, then, young sir, young lady.'

'Hard to say,' Wayland was saying as Leif pocketed the token again, 'at this end of time . . .'

'I guess so,' Megan said. 'Look, Wayland, we may be a while . . .'

'I'll be down in the marketplace then,' he said, 'or I won't.' He waved at them and set off through the gates again.

Leif threw Megan a briefly questioning glance as they followed the major-domo up through the castle door proper and a winding stairway that started making its way up around the walls of the central, circular tower. Megan shook her head, shrugged.

The second floor was one whole big airy room, rather like the keep in Minsar, except that all the tapestries seemed to have been taken down for the summer. With the weather here, fairly warm and pleasant this time of year, that was not a problem. The major-domo ushered them into the middle of the room, where there were a table and a chair, and in the chair, a man.

'Lord Fettick,' said Tald, 'these two travelers come on urgent business, bearing the sigil of Rod.'

The man in the chair looked up, somewhat surprised, then rose to greet them – old-fashioned courtesy, which Leif and Megan both answered with bows. 'Really? Then bring them a couple of chairs, please, and make them comfortable. And excuse yourself.'

Tald bustled about, bringing a couple of light ropewood chairs, which he placed on the far side of the table, and departed. The man gestured them to the chairs. Leif and Megan sat down.

Megan reflected that she had never actually met someone wearing rose-tinted glasses before, since she knew very few people who actually elected to wear glasses at all, the state of laser surgery being what it was. But here was Fettick, wearing them, a tall, slim, somewhat bemused-looking man in a gabardine, which was the height of style for the 14th century, but to Megan's eyes mostly looked like a cross between a monk's habit and a bathrobe. *It's probably pretty comfortable, though*, she thought.

If this was the High House's throne room, it wasn't overdecorated. Indeed, the throne was more of a comfy chair – a rather overstuffed one – and it was pulled up to what was probably usually used as a formal dining table, but was now in intensive use as a desk. The beautiful polished ebony surface was almost completely covered with all manner of paperwork and parchments and rolled-up books and sewn-up books, quills and pens and styli and tablets. It looked like an explosion in an old and eclectic library.

'Sir,' Leif said, 'thank you for taking the time to see us.'

'Well, you're welcome . . . briefly. I hope you understand I'm very busy this morning, and I don't have a lot of time . . .' He waved vaguely at the desk.

'We understand entirely,' said Leif. 'Sir, do you recognize this token?' He held up the golden coin that Rodrigues had given them.

Fettick fixed a somewhat skeptical look on it. 'Game

intervention,' he said softly, and whispered something to the computer. It whispered back, inaudibly.

His eyebrows went up. He whispered again. Then he said, 'Has Rod Almighty actually been *here*?'

'Yes, sir. We saw him last night. He sends his regards,' Leif said, which while not strictly true struck him as something Rod probably would have said.

'What did he want?'

'He wanted to talk to us about a matter which was concerning us . . . and that's why we've come to see you,' Leif said.

'Sir,' Megan said, 'your forces were in conflict with those of King Argath of Orxen not too long ago.'

'Yes.' Fettick sat down, and a small smile with a slightly feral edge crossed his face. Suddenly he didn't look quite so feckless. 'Yes, we won, didn't we?'

'Yes, you did. The problem right now, sir, is that anyone who fought a battle against Argath and won appears to be in danger of being – excuse me, I must use the indelicate word – "bounced." '

Fettick's eyes went wide for a moment. 'It *is* indelicate,' he said. And then he looked again at the pocket into which Leif had stuffed the token. 'Still, you have that . . . so I guess we can talk about such things as the Outside. Do you mean that the lady who got bounced the other day was—'

'She was about to have a battle with Argath. She would have won. She was bounced quite near the time when she would have begun fighting. Others have been, too – usually after the battle. But now this kind of thing seems to have started happening before the fact.'

'Is Argath responsible, or is it one of his people, or—'

'No one knows. All we've noticed is the connection. And so we're warning people who have fought with Argath recently, and come out the better, that they should look to their security. Here and elsewhere.'

'And take what kind of precautions?' said Fettick.

Leif and Megan looked at each other. 'Uh—' Megan said.

'Exercise more than usual care in your comings and goings,' Leif said. This drill he knew well enough, from his father's diplomatic connections. 'If you have routines in your travel or outside work, vary them. If you have trips scheduled that are really unnecessary, don't make them. Check out your living space, make sure there are no objects in it that you didn't put there, that you don't recognize . . .'

'Stay inside?' said Fettick. 'Opaque the windows? Lock the doors?'

Leif looked at him and thought maybe it might be wiser to be quiet for a moment.

Fettick sat in his chair again, laced his fingers over his robe. 'Young sir,' he said. 'Do you know what I do for my living . . . "out there?"'

Leif shook his head. He hadn't quarried that deeply into Fettick's background.

'I collect garbage,' said Lord Fettick, 'in Duluth, Minnesota. And my line of work requires that I repeat my routine flawlessly, twice a week, on each of three routes. "Varying" a garbage pickup route would be looked on, at the management levels above mine, with grave displeasure.' He sighed. 'And yes, I know how that lady was bounced the other night. It was tragic. Have you heard anything about how she's doing?'

'Still in hospital,' Leif said, 'and no news on when she might be likely to regain consciousness.'

'Yes. Well,' said Fettick. 'She was on her way to the store, I think, when someone came along and knocked her car off the road. I work in medium to heavy traffic all day, every day, and if someone wants to kill or maim me, believe me, they'll have no trouble doing it. My main concern is that they might miss me, and kill one of my workmates. And it sounds, from what you're telling me, that there's pretty much nothing that can be done to solve the problem at its root, at the moment; that those of us who're targeted have already committed the offense which has caused the targeting, and there's nothing we can do to make amends.'

'Probably not,' Leif said.

'That being the case,' said Lord Fettick, 'I can either spend the days from now until this person comes after me in a haze of fear, trying to protect myself against who knows what attack, from no one knows what direction – or I can get on with my life and refuse to be terrified. That's usually the way to deal with terrorists, isn't it?'

'While that is, ethically, a superior position,' Megan said softly, 'practically it sometimes has little effect on the terrorists, who count on something like it among proud or brave people. The terrorists have a nasty tendency to go ahead and try to blow you up anyway.'

'Well, let them come,' said Fettick. 'I'm going to sit

tight and do my job. There, and here.'

The tall slender man got up and came around his desk toward them. 'I'll tell you something for free,' he said. 'I've had it. Two nights, now, two nights of my good gameplay time, which costs me enough on my salary, Argath's miserable lackey the Duke has been in here making merry with his pestilent little dwarf, ogling my daughter, eating me out of house and home, drinking all my best wine, trying to make me think a dynastic marriage to him is a good idea. Nasty super-annuated creature. And here he's sat, these two nights, trying his best to blackmail me. Or worse, to browbeat me. Trying to sign me up for an alliance in which I have no interest, and one for which I would be condemned from one end of the Northeast to the other, an alliance with a man who attacked my country, attacked me, not eight months ago! The cheapest, nastiest kind of protection racket. And I have to sit here, and mouth platitudes at him for politics' sake – don't think I don't know at least that much about statecraft. I'm about up to here with pressure! I don't need a life like that. It's just not worth living.'

He sat back and sighed, looking down at the floor for a moment. 'I will take reasonable precautions,' he said. 'But no more. Whoever is behind this, I refuse to allow them to control my life. But I do thank you,' he said, 'for going out of your way to warn me. I take it there are other stops on your itinerary.'

'Yes,' Megan said. 'Duchess Morn—'

Fettick burst out laughing. 'You're going to bring *her* the same message you've brought *me*?'

'In essence,' said Megan.

'Do you have armor?'

She and Leif looked at each other. 'Are we likely to need it?'

'If you're going to tell her she has to vary her daily routine, you'll need a testudo at least,' Fettick said. 'Well, I wish you luck. I understand that you really do mean well . . . and if as I think you're somehow involved with the attempt to find out who has been bouncing people, I wish you all the luck you can use. Now I have to get on with things here. But are you sure you won't stay for breakfast?'

'Uh, no, sir,' Leif said. 'Thank you, though. We should get straight on to Duchess Morn's.'

'Sure you don't want to think twice about the armor?'

Leif smiled slightly. 'I think we'll manage.'

They bowed to Fettick and headed out.

They looked around in the marketplace, before making their transit, but found that Wayland had already left. No one was sure exactly when. 'Oh, well,' Leif said. 'We'll hear from him. Ready for transit?'

'Yup. Same size circle?'

'Same locus.'

'Ready. Cover your ears, we've got an altitude change—'

The world went black and white and phosphene-filled, and Megan swallowed to pop her ears, and swallowed again. They finally agreed to pop, and she looked down on a landscape as different from Errint as night from day. Everything in sight was flatland, a low swampy oxbowed river delta in which countless pools and trickles of water glittered and shone in the morning. Reeds stood up everywhere, and red-winged blackbirds and orioles perched on the reeds, swaying and singing in the wind that stroked through the reed-beds. In the center of everything was a great platform built on massive piles sunk into the water, and on the platform was a huge wooden house, turreted and towered like a castle. A wooden road was laid to it across the watery landscape, ending in a drawbridge and a steep switchback causeway that led up to the platform.

The two of them began to walk down the wooden path to the Duchess's castle. As they went, Megan slapped an opportunistic mosquito and said, 'Were you noticing Wayland this morning?'

'Huh? Not particularly.'

'Maybe it was just me,' Megan said, 'but there was something, a little, I don't know . . . a little "off" about him this morning. He seemed distracted somehow.'

'I noticed you distracting him, all right. Where did that come from?'

'It occurred to me that we might not want everybody and his brother to know about the token,' Megan said. 'For one thing, it's a good way to get it stolen. By the way, let me have it for a while?'

'Sure.' Leif handed it over.

'For another . . .' Megan trailed off. 'You notice the way he was answering questions?'

'No. Why?'

Megan shrugged. 'Just that I kept betting back these answers that were kind of general, or . . . I don't know . . . not really germane to what was said . . .'

'Maybe he has trouble hearing,' Leif said.

'Oh, come on.'

'No, seriously. If it's nerve damage causing the hearing problem, not even virtuality can do much about it, supposedly. He might not be hearing us right. I've seen that kind of thing happen with hearing aids.'

'Huh.' Megan thought about that. 'And it's not really something you'd ask about, I guess.'

'You sure you're not imagining it?'

Megan gave him a look, and then rubbed her eyes. She was feeling a little grainy around the edges, possibly from all the transits. 'Oh, I don't know . . . maybe I am. Or maybe he was just distracted. God knows *I* am at the moment. Anything's possible . . .' She sighed.

But just a little while later, as they walked, Megan thought about what she had said, and the answers she had gotten back, and finally she thought, *No. No, it was real enough. He's just a little off, somehow. Not concentrating . . . I guess anybody can be distracted, even when they're playing. Though for what people pay to play in here, you'd think they'd go get the distractedness out of their systems before they waste the money . . .*

She thought for a moment more, then said quietly, as they walked, 'Game intervention.'

'Listening.'

'Do you detect your boss's token here?'

'Concessionary token is detected. How can I help you?'

'The player called Wayland. Is he real or generated?'

'Do you mean, is the player human?'

'Yes.'

'Yes, the player is human.'

'Huh. Finished,' Megan said, and shoved the token back in her pocket. *I hate it when this computer tells me things I don't want to hear . . .*

'I see the guards up on the walls have noticed us,' Leif said. 'Look at all those crossbows . . .'

'Maybe *this* is what we really needed that armor for,' Megan said, as they came to the far end of the drawbridge, under the shadow of its gatehouses.

'Too late to go back now,' Leif said, entirely too cheerfully for someone who had so many weapons trained on him.

'I don't know,' Megan said softly, as guards began to pour down out of the gatehouses and onto the castle side of the drawbridge. 'Late breakfast is beginning to look real good . . .'

Megan stepped out of Sarxos into her personal space to find a pile of e-mail waiting – all kinds of things that needed to be handled, and she just wasn't up to it. Too many disappointments, too much excitement. Too many things hadn't worked . . .

She blinked herself out of the personal space, feeling intensely weary . . . and also feeling as if she had been hit over her body with a baseball bat. *Stress* . . . As she stood up from the chair, she glanced at the clock. 0516. *Ooooh . . . it can't be that late . . . can it?*

Yes, it can . . .

Megan left the office and went off into the kitchen, groaning a little as she moved. Somebody had thoughtfully left her tea-making things out, and a banana on the counter.

Dad, she thought, and smiled slightly. *Bananas are good for all-nighters*, he always said. *The potassium helps keep your brain working.* And since he pulled so many all-nighters himself, he would know . . .

There had been fewer repercussions regarding Megan's skipping 'family night' than she had feared. Her dad had clearly understood that something important was going on. He had apparently spoken to her mom about it as well, and hadn't asked Megan any questions about it . . . which was kind of him, and typical. But there would be questions today, all right. She was going to have to explain what was going on . . . and she dreaded that. She knew that what she hadn't told Winters, her dad would quickly deduce, and he would tell her to forget about the bouncing problems in Sarxos, and let Net Force handle it. If he told her that, she would have to do what he said. Megan respected him that much, at least.

Still . . .

She put the kettle on the stove and turned the burner on under it, peeled the banana, and sat down at the kitchen table, eating reflectively. For about the tenth time she began going over again, in her head, the lines of investigation she and Leif had been following. It was hard to think, though. She was really tired, and the image of Duchess Morn, laughing at them uproariously, kept intruding.

She and Leif hadn't exactly needed armor to deal with her. Maybe Fettick had been overstating that end of things. But Morn's good-natured scorn at the idea that someone might be about to bounce *her* was like enough to Fettick's to be its twin. Morn was in her seventies, little and skinny and tough as old boot leather, and intensely funny. *Fierce*, Megan thought. She found herself wishing that when she hit seventy, she could be something like that.

'Let them try to get me,' had been Morn's attitude about the whole thing. She was satisfied that her computer was secure enough, that her life was well-enough protected. But even if it hadn't been, Megan thought, Morn had the total fearlessness of someone who reckons that she's lived her life well, for a long time, and was not afraid to 'check out' if that was the card which fell in front of her when the next deal came along. Megan and Leif had gone away from Woodhouse with their ears full of an old lady's amused scolding of those who had the nerve to intrude in her personal business. And then both of them had to get out of Sarxos, because school was coming up later in the day, and they were both dead tired, though they hated to admit it to each other.

'I've had a long day,' Megan had said to Leif. 'But I may be back in here later. Leave Chris's token with me, okay?'

'No problem,' Leif had said. He'd handed it to her and disappeared, looking as tired as Megan felt, and more dejected.

So there the thing sat, in on her 'desk' in her virtual

workspace. Now, as she finished the banana and the kettle started shrieking, Megan got up hurriedly to shut it up, and thought about the token again.

Which of the six could it be? Sherlock Holmes was whispering in her ear: *eliminate the impossible, and what you have left is the truth.* Or at least possible.

Five-thirty. I can't believe I was in there all night. But . . . She raised her eyebrows, sighed at herself, poured boiling water into her teacup, then went into the small bathroom off the kitchen, wetted a washcloth with cold water and just plastered it over her eyes for a moment. The chill of it on her face was something of a shock, a welcome one.

Megan let it rest there for a moment, and looked at the faint lights moving inside her eyelids, phosphene byproducts of how tired her eyes were. Then she peeled the washcloth off, left it by the sink, and went in to get her tea.

Megan sat down, sipped at it gingerly, and started to go over things one more time. She couldn't get rid of the feeling that she'd missed something about the server logs. But then Leif seemed to think they'd exploited everything they could from examining that set of information, and she was willing enough to bow to his expertise in this area. *There must be something else,* she thought. *Something we've missed . . .*

But the back of her mind kept going back to the server logs, and wouldn't be appeased. *It's just brain fugue,* Megan thought to herself after a while, sipping at the tea again, and burning herself again. *I'm like a rat going down a tunnel with no cheese in it, again and again.* It was the same kind of behavior she made fun of in her mother when her mother put the car keys down and later couldn't find them, and kept checking the same spot over and over and over, even though she knew perfectly well by now that they weren't there . . . *I'm no better than she is.*

The tea was beginning to cool enough to drink. Megan sipped at it one more time. *I feel so grungy. What'm I going to wear to school today? I haven't checked the laundry situation in days . . .*

. . . Then she swore softly, got up again, and headed straight back into the office.

She went over to the desk, pushed yet another pile of books off to one side – *Baedeker's Handbook for London, 1875? . . . Fungi of the World? Taste of the East? . . . what, he wants to go back in* time *for a curry now? With mushrooms in it, I guess . . .* and sat down in the implant chair again, lined the implant up.

There was Rhea's ochre surface spread out before her, all powdered blue with new-blown snow from one of the nearby methane vents, and there was Saturn hanging golden and uncommunicative in the long cold darkness, like a message delivered and unread. *All that e-mail . . .* Megan thought. 'Computer? Chair, please.' The chair appeared. 'Show me what's come in.'

The icons of about fifteen messages appeared in the air before her, some holding still, some rotating gently, some vibrating up and down as an indication of their urgency. The urgent ones were in the minority – though, as Megan read through the mail, she found once again that other people's definitions of urgency didn't usually match hers. Two more mails from Carrie Henderson, who really really wanted her to do something that Megan didn't bother finishing listening to. Yet another unnecessary notice about the SAT's. Someone selling subscriptions to a new virtual news service, a demo account of which began playing itself noisily in one corner of her space, showing her a smoke-filled expanse stitched with the burning lines of battlefield lasers, a firefight going on in some dark place in Africa. She wished she had a hammer to hit the sender with. Instead, Megan just told the machine to turn the demo off, and went back to reducing the clutter, icon by icon.

Several failed connects of attempted live chat . . . Well, she routinely refused chat while she was in Sarxos. *J. Simpson? . . . Who's that? . . .* She shook her head. You did sometimes get requests to chat from people you'd never seen or heard of before. Probably it was someone she'd run into in the game who wanted to follow up on something.

She opened the messages, but they had nothing but the characteristic 'failed message, chat refused' tag inside them. Oh, well, Megan thought. As her mother usually said, if it was important, they'd call back. If it wasn't important, they'd call back . . .

Maybe whoever this is left some mail inside Sarxos, Megan thought. 'Computer? Sarxos log-in.'

'Working.'

Her own area didn't go away, but went shadowy while the Sarxos logo and copyright notices displayed themselves burning in the air before her as usual, and her scores and last-play times came up. 'Resume from previous extraction point?' said the computer. 'Or start new area play?'

'Another alternative.'

'State it, please.'

'Do you recognize this token?' She picked up Rodrigues's golden sigil, tossed it in her hand.

'Concessionary token recognized. How can I help you?'

Down the same old tunnel, Megan thought, resigned. 'Identify attempted chat connections to my account from 1830 local last night to 0515 today.'

A moment's silence. 'No connections from within Sarxos.'

'Okay.' *J. Simpson* . . . She shook her head. 'Any e-mail waiting?'

'No e-mail.'

So Wayland had come up with nothing new. 'I want access to server logs,' Megan said.

'That access is allowed with your token. Which logs would you like to see?'

'Logs for players Rutin, Walse, Hunsal, Orieta, Balk the Screw, and Lateran.'

'Specify mode. Audio? Text? Graphical?'

'Graphics, please,' Megan said. Her eyes weren't up to reading much text at the moment.

'What span of time?'

'The last—' Megan waved her hand, not really caring, '—four months.'

'Working.'

Six separate bar graphs stacked themselves up in the air in front of Megan, looking something like a long detailing of what the Dow Jones index might have been doing for the last quarter. Each upright bar was a twenty-four hour period: in it, as a series of bright vertical dashes stitched down the darker 'bar,' was a representation of the number of hours that the person in question had been in Sarxos, playing.

The six players were serious ones. Not one of them seemed to have played less than four hours a day, for all four months. Some of them had played six, or eight, routinely. Some of them had repeated stretches, especially at weekends or around holidays, when they were in the game for fourteen hours a day, or more. *I wonder where they've been getting their massage programs from*, Megan thought, stretching her aching body. *Jeez, I thought I was fairly serious about the game. But these people are* obsessed.

For amusement, she said to the computer, 'Put up the matching server log for Brown Meg.'

It came up. She breathed out a rueful laugh. Over the last few days, her usage, staggered as it was, had become almost as obsessive as theirs. *Dad's gonna have words with me*, she thought. *And as for Mom . . . no, let's not even think about it right now.*

'Display matching server usage for Leif Hedgewizard,' Megan said. Another bar graph appeared below hers. His usage looked a lot like hers, for the past few days. *He's no better . . .*

And there was the tunnel, still with no cheese in it. She made a face at herself, and said, 'Oh, go on, display server usage for Lateran.'

It came up. Lateran was as bad as any of them. Worse. Another mad one, in and out constantly. 'Display usage for Argath.'

Argath, strangely, wasn't in as much as Megan would have thought: his usage over the past several months actually looked more like *her* usual pattern, though it had been busier than usual the past few days. It didn't seem normal, somehow . . . but then, what *was* normal usage for a Sarxos player? *Was* there any such thing? Probably not.

Megan raised her eyebrows at the thought, and said to the computer, 'Display usage pattern for – oh, Wayland—'

His pattern came up under Argath's. Megan sipped at her tea again, which she had 'brought' into the virtual space with her, and sat gazing a little blearily at all the bar graphs hanging there glowing in the air in front of her. *I should go out and do the cold-washcloth trick again*, she thought, blinking.

And then she stopped, and looked at the graphs again: not the way she normally would have, but with her eyes squinted shut a little bit, as they had been before.

Lateran's graph looked a lot like Wayland's.

In the general patterning, the way the dashes and blank spaces fell . . . there were a lot more dashes, times 'in,' than there were empty space. Lateran's graph made Megan wonder a little more as she looked at each twenty-four hour period and realized how much of it was taken up by gameplay. Most of it. A whole *lot* of it. And if you compared the end of one day with the beginning of the next – as often as not, they ran right into one another. *Well, midnight. Peak game-time, after all—*

But that wasn't it. *Twelve-hour stretches. Fourteen, sixteen sometimes.* The pattern repeated, cycling backward very slowly through the four-month period. Six hours in, twenty minutes out. Eight hours in, one hour out. Two hours in, an hour out. Five hours in—

The pattern definitely repeated. And Lateran's timings were beyond 'obsessed.' They were positively pathological. *When does he sleep?* Megan wondered. *More to the point, when does he* work? *Even if you worked at home, you'd have a hard time keeping up a schedule like this. Without getting fired, anyway . . .*

'Computer—'

'Listening.'

'User profile on player Lateran.'

'Your concessionary token does not allow that access. Please consult with Chris Rodrigues for further information.'

'What time is it for Chris Rodrigues?' Megan said.

'0242.'

He's on the West Coast somewhere. I'm not going to wake him up at quarter of three in the morning. Unless— 'Is Chris in the game at the moment?'

'No.'

I'll have to wait . . . She looked again at Lateran's server log. *If this person has a job, it has to be done at home. But even if it is, it can't be more than part-time . . . not with this kind of usage . . . And it's not a child.* Sarxos' age limit, because of the violence, was sixteen and up. *So Lateran has to either be in school or some kind of work* . . . She shook her head. The usage didn't make sense.

And Megan looked down at Wayland's usage. It really was *very* much like Lateran's. Six hours on, two hours off . . . eight hours on, two hours off . . . seven hours on . . . And the pattern repeated, and cycled slowly backward through the four-month period. *They're a little out of synch. Not exactly alike, but* . . . She shook her head.

But the strange way that Wayland had sounded this morning was still on Megan's mind. A very peculiar suspicion began to grow in her. It was impossible, of course, because Wayland's server log and Lateran's server log showed them as often being on line at the same time . . . but you couldn't play two characters at once.

Could you?

'Computer,' Megan said.

'Listening.'

'Maximum number of characters played by any one Sarxos user.'

'Thirty-two.'

'What's the user's name?'

'That information is not available to you with your present concessionary token. Please consult Chris Rodrigues for further information.'

'Yeah, yeah. Access the records of player Lateran.'

'Records accessed: holding in store.'

'How many other characters does the person playing Lateran play?'

'Five.'

'Is one of them "Wayland"?'

Silence for a moment: then, 'Yes.'

Megan flushed hot and then cold with the confirmation. 'Listen,' she said, as a whole group of horrible possibilities started opening up on front of her: now her job was to start limiting them— 'With this token, can I access Chris Rodrigues's file of attempted and successful bounces on Sarxos players?'

'That access is allowed.'

'Access the file, please, and hold it in store.'

'Done.'

'Display the bounce periods on a similar bar graph. Star each one.'

The computer did so: each bright star of a bounce 'timing' was superimposed on a dark translucent bar corresponding to the graphs above.

'Pull down the graphs for Lateran and Wayland. Superimpose them on the bounce chart.'

Obediently, the computer did so. All the bounces, including the latest one with Elblai, fell inside time periods when both Wayland and Lateran were reported to be in the game.

But it's impossible, Megan thought, horror and triumph beginning to rise in her together. *It's impossible. Both those logs for Wayland and Lateran can't be true. They can't both be there at once. But if one of them was—*

'Computer!'

'Listening.'

'Is it possible for a player to play two characters at once during the same game period?'

'Only sequentially. Simultaneous play of multiple characters has been ruled out by the designer and is illegal in the system.'

They're the same player. They're both there at the same time. They can't be. *And the computer hasn't noticed, because it's not trained to notice.*

Someone's found a way to fake being in the system.

'It's too important . . .' she whispered. 'Computer, I need to talk to Chris Rodrigues, right now. This is an emergency.'

There was a moment's silence, and the computer said, 'Chris is not answering his page. Please try again later.'

'This is an *emergency*,' Megan said. 'Don't you understand me?'

'The system understands "emergency",' the computer said, 'but has no authority from a concessionary token of the type presently in your possession to contact him at this time. Please try again later.'

It's him, she thought. *The bouncer. It's* him.

Oh, shit . . .!

'Do you wish to leave a message for Chris Rodrigues?'

Megan opened her mouth, then shut it again as another thought occurred. 'No,' she said.

'What other services do you require?'

Megan sat there looking at all those bar graphs. 'Show me the other server logs,' she said, 'the same period, for all the other characters played by the player who plays Wayland and Lateran.'

'Working.' Three more graphs appeared: the first and the third very closely matched the patterns of

Wayland's and Lateran's. There were some minor differences in the timing, and the patterns were slightly more elaborate: but again, these characters spent too much time in the system to be realistic, and again, they cycled slowly backwards over the four-month period. *Automatic,* Megan thought. *No question of it.*

The middle usage-graph looked more real. Three hours in, twenty hours out. Four hours in, thirty-five hours out . . . a more scanty usage pattern. Not a dillie, but not obsessed, either.

Megan let her eyes go unfocused again, a good way to make sure you were seeing the pattern you thought you were. The similarities were too strong among all the questionable graphs to possibly be a coincidence.

'Store display,' Megan said.

'File name?'

'Megan-and-Leif-One. Can I copy this display to e-mail?'

'Yes.'

'Copy to player Leif Hedgewizard.'

'Done: holding for pickup.'

'Copy it to him out of the system as well.'

'Message dispatched to the Net at 0554 local.'

Now *what do I do? . . .*

Megan swallowed, had to do it again. Her mouth was dry. *Lateran. We were right. I know we were right. The new up-and-coming young general . . .* She smiled a little grimly. *Something of an analyst. And something of a danger, to judge by this. Anyone who could invent a way to fool a virtual-reality system into thinking they were there when they* weren't . . .

More to the point, Megan thought. *Why would they waste the technique in here? It's only a game.* True, there were people who felt that Sarxos was a life-or-death matter, who spent almost all their waking hours in it, who lived it and slept it and ate it and drank it and, as Chris said, wanted to move in. But this, though . . . Megan shook her head. *This is someone willing to use, or possibly invent, a technology whose whole purpose is to exploit the basic issue of presence in a virtual environment.*

She had always believed that the 'fingerprint' you left in the Net by your presence with an implant attached was indelible and uncounterfeitable. It was one of the truisms on which safe use of the Net was built: that you were who your implant said you were, that you were *where* you claimed to be, *when* you claimed to be. The implant hooked to your own physicality supposedly made authentification of your actions in the Net final and certain. But somebody – Wayland? Lateran? Whoever this person really was – had found a way to be 'there' when they *weren't* there. While their genuine physicality was somewhere else, doing something else. Breaking into someone's house and smashing their computer . . . running a middle-aged grandmother off the road and into a pole.

What next?

And all for the sake of a game.

Or was that *all* it was? For the implications of such technology were horrific.

Megan shuddered, swallowed again, her mouth still dry. *There's still no proof. This is still circumstantial evidence.*

But it's real good circumstantial evidence, and it's gonna raise a lot of questions.

Now what?

To the computer, she said, 'Store the graphs . . . remove them from my workspace.'

'Done.'

Megan sat and looked at Saturn out of the window.

He'll know, of course. We told him to his face, what we were investigating, what our suspicious were. Even about Lateran. He knows we're onto him.

It's not Fettick and Morn we should be worried about. It's us.

And it's not like we're that hard to find, either, Megan thought. *Schedules that we don't vary. Known addresses.* She smiled a wry smile.

I need to get hold of Winters right now. But—

And then she stopped.

What was in her mind was the image of Wayland, Lateran, whoever ran him – coming here, coming after her. Or coming after Leif. It was all too easy to get addresses and phone numbers and all kinds of 'personal' information off the Net. But at the same time—

Why do I need to worry? Megan thought, her mouth starting to undry itself a little. *We've got the standard number of defensive firearms here, and I know how to use them all. Someone comes up to me in the street, or tries to get physical with me—* She smiled grimly. *No, I think I'd like to hand this one – we'd like to hand this one – to Winters, on a plate.*

Why not? And come to think of it . . . why should I just sit here waiting for it to happen?

She looked again thoughtfully at those attempted chat contacts. *J. Simpson*, she thought. *Where are you, J. Simpson?*

'Sarxos computer,' she said. 'Thank you. Log out.'

'You're welcome, Brown Meg. Enjoy your day.' The copyright notice came and went in a flash of crimson.

'Computer,' Megan said. 'Access e-mail address for J. Simpson. Open new mail . . .'

And she smiled.

Leif popped into his stave-house workspace and sat down on the Danish Modern couch, rubbing his eyes. 'Mail?' he said to his computer.

'Loads of it, oh my lord and master. How do you want it? Important first? Dull first? In order of receipt?'

'Yeah, the last,' Leif said, and rubbed his eyes again. He felt deathly tired.

He had thought he would sleep like a log (however logs slept) when he got out of Sarxos last night. But instead he tossed, and turned, and couldn't get settled. Something was bothering him, something he couldn't identify, something he'd missed.

Not Lateran. Sukin syn, *it's not Lateran . . .* He couldn't get rid of the thought. And he was thinking about Wayland too. What Megan had been saying. 'A "canned" quality . . .'

An e-mail about some event his mother wanted him to attend was playing. 'Look,' he said to the machine, 'put it all on hold for a moment.'

'Okay.'

Leif thought back to other encounters he had had

with Wayland, right back to the very first ones he'd had with him. The man had seemed a little eccentric . . . but you got that with people in Sarxos, sometimes. The more Leif thought about those conversations, though, the more what Megan had said began to ring true. And a player could play back his own experiences, if he'd thought to save them . . .

Leif smiled grimly. He was something of a packrat, and tended to archive everything, until his father started complaining that there was no room left in the machine for business. 'Listen,' he said, 'get my Sarxos archives.'

'Their machine's on the line, boss,' said his own computer, 'and the things it's saying about you, I wouldn't want to repeat. The *storage* space you use—!'

'Yeah, I pay for it. Never mind. Listen, I want to hear all the conversations I've had with the character "Wayland." '

'Right you are.'

He started listening. By the third conversation, he had already begun to pick up repetitions of phrases. Not just because they were familiar – but because they were spoken in exactly the same intonation every time. The hair began to rise on the back of his neck. Another phrase: 'Now that is very interesting.' Repeated again, a couple of months later: 'Now that is very interesting.' The very same intonation. And a third time: perfect, the same timing, to the second.

But then . . . he played the record of his and Megan's conversation with Wayland. 'Now that is very interesting . . .'

A different intonation. Much more amused . . . and definitely more aware.

He swallowed, and looked up at something vibrating just off to one side. It was one of the pieces of e-mail . . . and it had Megan's address on it.

'Dammit. Open that!' he said to the computer.

It did. Leif found himself looking at a series of stacked bar graphs. They were people's server logs, compared by time. They were—

His mouth fell open as he looked at the last logs at the bottom of the stack: two sets, superimposed over one another, and the stars, the timings of all the bounces there had been in the last few months, laid over them.

Leif's throat seized. He couldn't even swear. There were no words bad enough for what he saw there.

It was *Lateran.*

And Lateran is Wayland, too. And Wayland is "canned", somehow. We've been hearing preprogrammed phrases . . .

Except last night. *Now this is very interesting . . .* and Wayland's smile.

Where's Megan?!

He didn't have her voice comm-code. They'd never needed it, all their contacts had been through the Net.

'Computer! Get Megan on chat—'

'She's not available, boss.'

'Log in to Sarxos. Look for her there.'

He waited through intolerable seconds while the machine logged in, while the logo and the copyright notices displayed. After a moment, his machine said, 'Not there, boss.'

He couldn't find out when she'd last been there, either, because he didn't have the token. She had it.

With the weight of the information in front of him, the data that she now had – with the memory of their meeting last night with Wayland, the information that he now knew *they* had – and the fact that Leif couldn't find her – it all came together, and suddenly Leif knew what had happened: what, if he was lucky, was just now happening.

Then he started to swear, calling first Megan, and then Wayland, things in Russian that would doubtless have sent his mother straight up the wall if she'd heard them. He was seized with the complete helplessness of being virtual when you desperately needed to be concrete: his total inability to be in Washington, right then, when he was actually stuck in New York.

Leif shouted at the computer, 'James Winters! Net Force emergency! Immediate connect!'

A slightly bleary voice said, 'Winters—'

Leif gasped for breath, and then shouted:

'HELP!'

She sent the e-mail, and she waited . . . and nothing happened. *Some sensible person is still asleep,* she thought. *Why not?*

Finally Megan gave up on waiting. It was getting late. She went upstairs and had her shower, and got dressed, keeping as quiet as she could because her dad had plainly been up late, working in some other room besides the office, and had turned in. Her mom, as so often happened, was already gone. The brothers hadn't stayed over, last night – one had med-surg nursing rounds early the next morning, and the other had been complaining about an impending final exam in a course called Advanced Stressed Concrete 302. They had both made themselves scarce after dinner.

She came down again, thought about another cup of tea, decided against it. There was nothing happening at school today that would really be important . . . but that was no reason not to go. All her schoolwork was ready. The portable was charged up, all the necessary data solids carrying her reference texts were in her bag. And her ride's horn went, outside.

Megan grabbed the bag and the portable, dropped her keycard in her pocket, slapped the front door to lock-behind, and breezed out, heard the door clock closed and the lock set, tested it to make sure it was shut tight, turned—

—and simply found him there, standing in front of her, reaching out with something black in his hand.

Reflex saved Megan, nothing else. She flung herself off to one side as he grabbed for her, and threw her bag at him, knocking him back a little. Megan felt the subdued hiss and sizzle of a body-field deranger close by. One solid touch and her bioelectricity would go briefly crazy, enough to drop her where she stood, 'shorted out.' The thing's effective range was about four feet. Megan hit the ground rolling, rolled to her feet, got up and danced away from the man across the front lawn, intent on keeping him far away from her. He dashed at her again, and again Megan backed off, though it really annoyed her to do so.

Half of her was scared out of her wits. The rest of her was absorbed in the business of the dance. *Don't let him close, stay out of range* – and behind, in her brain, a leisurely running commentary seemed to be going on. *Heard the horn, where's your ride, that's not the right car, same make though, maybe even same year, how did he—*

—how long had he suspected that she and Leif were on his trail? How closely had he been watching them? *Leif*, she thought, *why didn't I—!*

The man jumped at her again, not speaking. She almost wished that he would shout, would say something. *About five foot nine*, said another part of the mind, clinical: *medium build, gray sweatshirt, jeans, black loafers, white socks* – white socks?? *Jeez* – *big nose. Mustache. Eyes* – *eyes*— She couldn't tell the color from here, and she wasn't going to get close enough to find out – *big hands, very big hands*: a face surprisingly slack and still for all the action they were going through, dancing around on the lawn at seven-forty-five in the morning, *and why isn't anyone noticing this, why aren't the neighbors—?!* Megan opened her mouth to scream as loudly as she could—

And then she realized that he had thrown away the deranger, and had something else in his hand, with which he was taking aim—

She never felt the blast from the sonic hit her. The next thing she knew, she was lying on the ground and couldn't move a muscle in her body. All this was making something of a mockery of all the training she'd had, all the good advice from her self-defense instructor. Locked out of the house, nowhere to run, no time to get away, no *time*—

The man leaned over her, the face not quite expressionless – just somewhat annoyed at the trouble she had caused him – as he started to pick her up, haul her up to a vaguely seated position, preparatory, she knew, to him picking her up and putting her in that car to take her away. *Never let an attacker take you* anywhere, one of her self-defense instructors had said, in a tone more urgent than she could remember him ever having used before. *The only reason someone wants to take you somewhere is to make you a hostage, or to rape or kill you in private. Make them do it in public, if they're going to do it. It may be awful, but it's better than being dead*—

Do something, she said to her throat, her lungs. *Scream! Big breath, now scream!* But the big breath just would not come in, and the scream came out 'huh, huh.' The scream was all in her head, only in her head, and Megan was briefly lost in a paroxysm of rage and fear, but only briefly, because, this was strange, the scream was in the air over her head—

The man looked up, startled at the dark shape dropping toward him like a stone from the sky. He glanced down at Megan again, his eyes just briefly narrowed with intent, moved his hand—

—and then fell sideways, hard, next to her and partly on top of her. She heard the awful thick thud as his head hit the ground. It had been dry, the lawn was fairly brown and the ground was hard—

Megan fell back, staring straight up. She couldn't turn her head, could only hear the scream of the engine, the ringing in her ears. And then could have broken right down and wept, though not with fear, of course not, with relief, at the sound of all the footsteps all around her, at the sight, just out of the corner of one eye, of the beautiful black Net Force craft with its gold stripe down the side, and the police craft landing behind it—

—and the sight of James Winters suddenly looming above her, and saying to the medical people, 'She's okay, thank God, she just took some sonic, come on, give her a hand. And as for *him*—'

He looked down past the narrowing cone of vision that was all Megan had left at the moment. 'Here's our bouncer,' said Winters, in a voice fierce with anger and satisfaction. 'Lock him up.'

It took several days for the excitement to die down. Megan spent some of them in the hospital – sonics are not something you just walk away from – eventually talking to the police and to the Net Force people who came by to see her, including Winters, and to Leif, who came down from New York.

Everyone was treating her very gently, as if she might break. For the first day, she didn't mind it so much. The second day, it was only occasionally annoying. But by the third day, it began to get on her nerves, and she said so, forcefully, to several different people. Even Winters, finally.

'She'll be all right,' she heard him say to the nurse outside her door as he headed off. He turned, pointed at her. 'But the day you get out of here – you, and him—' He pointed at Leif. 'My office, ten o'clock.'

'I'll be in New York,' Leif said hopefully.

'What, is your computer broken? Ten o'clock.'

And he was gone.

Megan sat back in the comfortable chair in the corner – they'd let her out of bed at this point – and said to Leif, 'Were the Net Force people in with you this morning?'

'Yeah.'

'Did they give you any more technical detail on how they thought Mister Simpson, or Wallace, or Duvalier—' he had several aliases, it turned out – 'was managing to fool the system into thinking he wasn't there when he was, and vice versa?'

Leif shook his head. 'I have to confess, I'm not real strong on the technical side of it. He apparently had a second implant which he had somehow taught to fake being connected to his body. Don't ask me how you do that . . . *they're* apparently real interested. And he had it running an "expert program," an aware-system routine—'

Leif leaned on the windowsill. 'This is real old stuff. You ever hear of a program called RACTER? One of my uncles knew the guy who wrote it.'

Megan shook her head.

'The name was short for "Raconteur," ' Leif said. 'It was a descendant of those old Turing-test programs, the ones meant to fake being human, enough to pass in conversation, anyway. RACTER was meant to convince you that you were shooting the breeze with somebody, just casually. Simpson, or whatever his name is, had done a tailored "aware" program for

Sarxos, one that could hold moderately good conversations with people in his persona . . . and get away with it. It's no surprise it worked, I guess. You just automatically assume, when you're in Sarxos, that whoever you're talking to is either a real player, or generated by the game itself . . . and sometimes game-generated people do act up a little bit. Even Sarxos has bugs, after all . . . And it looks like our guy had four of these programs running, sometimes all at once. The fifth "self" would be him, turning up here and there, servicing the various personas to make sure that everyone thought they were who they were supposed to be . . . while he went about the rest of his business: being Lateran, and getting rid of the people who he thought were getting in Lateran's way, one by one.'

'Do they have any idea why he bounced Elblai so hard?'

Leif shook his head. 'The police psychiatrists have been talking to him, but I think the general feeling is that Elblai just put too much pressure on him. He cracked. He might have been going that way for a while. Shel had been putting a lot of pressure on him . . . but not as much as Elblai did. It just all got too much for him . . . But he'd been very careful, very canny. Covering his tracks for a long time . . . lots more than four months, apparently.' Leif made a bemused face. 'I don't think anything the shrinks can come up with is going to help him when he comes to trial, though. Hit and run, attempted manslaughter, various burglaries and destruction of property, and in your case, attempted murder . . . I doubt we'll see him in

Sarxos again any time soon. Or anywhere else . . .'

Leif looked at her, folding his arms and turning away from the window. 'I'm just glad you're okay,' he said.

'Yeah, well, if it weren't for you, I might not *be* okay.'

'I was terrified that I was going to be too late . . .'

'I thought that I might be about to be late, too,' Megan said, 'in the less usual sense of the word. Look . . . let's just forget it. There are more important things to worry about now.'

'Oh?'

'The day after tomorrow,' Megan said, 'at ten o'clock . . .'

When the hour came, Megan and Leif were sitting, virtually, in James Winters's office. But not being there physically did not make their presence any more comfortable for them.

His desk was neat. There were a couple of tidy piles of printouts laid in front of him, a couple of data storage solids off to one side. Winters looked up from the paperwork, and his face was very cool.

'I need to talk to you two a little bit,' he said, 'about responsibility.'

They both sat mute. It didn't seem like a good time to argue the point.

'I had conversations with both of you regarding this problem,' he said. 'Do you remember those conversations?'

'Uh, yes,' Megan said.

'Yes,' said Leif.

Winters looked particularly closely at Megan. 'Are

you *sure* you remember it, now? Because your actions since then are such as to suggest that you had a profound incident of amnesia. I'd be really tempted to suggest that your parents take you down to the NP center at Washington U for the purpose of what my father, in the ancient days, would have called "having your head felt." If you can demonstrate some physical pathology to support the way you acted, it would make my life a whole lot easier.'

Megan's face positively simmered with embarrassment.

'No, huh? I was afraid not. *Why* did you not do as I requested?' Winters said. 'Granted, it wasn't an order; you're not under my orders . . . but normally, requests of this kind from a senior Net Force official to a Net Force Explorer can be considered as having some force.'

Megan looked at the floor, swallowed. 'I thought the situation wasn't as dangerous as you thought it was,' she said finally, looking up again. 'I thought Leif and I could handle it.'

'The thought didn't possibly cross your mind that you would like to really look good?'

'Uh. Yes. Yes, it did.'

'And what about you?' Winters said to Leif.

'Yes,' Leif said. 'I thought we could handle it. And I thought it would be really neat to handle this ourselves, before the senior members got involved.'

'So.' Winters looked at him.' You weren't thinking of sparing us danger, or trouble, not specifically.'

'No.'

'Time, maybe,' Megan said.

'And glory?' Winters said softly.

'. . . A little,' said Leif.

Winters sat back. 'You two are nothing if not an easy debrief . . . Well, I've had time to look over all the logs. There's no question of your tenacity. And I have to say I smell dedication here. Got your teeth into it, didn't you?'

'I didn't want to let go,' Megan said.

'We started a job,' Leif said softly. 'When you spoke to us . . . we weren't finished. We wanted to finish.'

Winters sat still, looking down at the paper on his desk. He reached out to the corner of the stack, riffled the many pages. 'There has been a certain amount of pressure from above,' he said, 'to simply chuck you two out of the Explorers as a liability. The example of recklessness and disrespect for authority which your actions of the last few days suggest is not thought to be a good one for the rest of the Explorers. Because news will get out about what happened – it always gets out – and there's concern that other Explorers, in their youth and inexperience, will start thinking that this kind of behavior might actually be appropriate. We've managed to do a certain amount of damage limitation, but—' He rolled his eyes. 'That little scene on your front lawn did not help, Megan. Details of what happened, and what you were involved with, are invariably going to leak out. I'm hoping for your sakes that there are no legal repercussions. When you're doing what we've suggested you do, we have some slight power to protect you. When you're *not*—'

Winters glanced at the ceiling as if asking silently for

help, and shook his head. 'Meanwhile, I have to figure out what to do with you . . . because there's pressure being brought to bear on us from more than one source. There are people in this organization who tell me that the analysis which brought you to your conclusions was a nice piece of lateral thinking, and they would look forward to working with you at some later date. And if I throw you out now, that's going to make that option fairly difficult. Yet at the same time, there are other people shaking their heads and saying, "Throw them the hell out!" So what do I do? Any suggestions?'

He looked at them. Leif opened his mouth, shut it again. 'Go ahead,' said Winters. 'I don't see how you can make it any worse for yourself than it already is.'

'Keep us on,' Leif said, 'but on probation.'

'What does probation look like to you?'

'I'm not sure.'

'You?' Winters looked at Megan. 'Any ideas?'

'Only a question.' She swallowed. 'What happens to full Net Force professionals when they do this kind of thing?'

'Mostly they get cashiered,' Winters said grimly. 'Only extraordinary extenuating circumstances sometimes manage to save them. Can you suggest any in your case?'

'That we've uncovered possibly one of the most dangerous trends in thirty years' worth of virtual experience?' Leif said, just a touch innocently.

Winters looked at him sidelong, and allowed out just one thin grudging smile. Leif saw it and knew, instantly, that they had him, that it was going to be all right. Not comfortable . . . but all right.

'That is, fortunately for you, true,' Winters said. 'Up until now, the whole virtuality system has been predicated on the certainty that transactions carried out remotely via implant were genuine. Now suddenly all that is thrown into confusion. There's hardly a part of the Net that this doesn't touch. All authentication protocols everywhere are going to have to be looked at, made proof against the kind of subversion that your Sarxonian friend managed to devise. With whose help, we're not sure . . . but it's being looked into. Sarxos has been a testing-ground for some technologies that various countries are interested in. When someone starts interfering with that particular game . . . well, alarm bells ring. They'll ring for a long time. But leaving that aside for the moment, this incident has been a wake-up call for a lot of people who felt their systems were secure. Sarxos has a very highly thought-of proprietary security system. The discovery that it was being subverted in this manner, filled with spurious data, and no one suspected that this had been going on for months, perhaps *many* months . . . it came as quite a shock . . . If Sarxos could be subverted this way, so could many other carefully built proprietary systems. Banking systems. Securities clearing systems. "Smart" systems that handle various aspects of national security for nations around the world. Weapons control systems . . .' Winters trailed off. 'It doesn't bear thinking about, the amount of redesign that's going to have to be done. Except that we have to think about it now, thanks to you.' The narrow smile went crooked. 'There are probably more managers and systems analysts and hardware and software jockeys cursing your names at the moment than you'll ever have again, if you're lucky. And the same people are blessing you. If you were to die right now, no telling which direction you'd go.'

He sat back. 'Meanwhile . . . Sarxos itself—' He picked up one of the pieces of paper from the top of the stack, looked at it, put it aside. 'Sarxos has possibly just survived as a company because of what you've done. It's been a major profit-maker for its parent firm, and the attack on that player, along with the inability to catch the person who did it, was beginning to affect the company's performance in the market. The Law of the Market is "Know when they're greedy, know when they're scared . . ." Sarxos's stockholders got scared, and the market started losing confidence in the company. Their stock's value plummeted all over the world, everywhere it traded. Now, the game's designer, who is a man not exactly without some political pull due to being at least half a Croesus's worth of rich, has asked us to give you every possible consideration in what you do. The parent company's CEO has weighed in on your side, an astonishing event for a man who was widely thought not to care if the Big Bad Wolf was about to eat his grandmother unless at the time she happened to be carrying a bag full of his stock options. The police in Bloomington are very happy with you, because your suspect's testimony has led them straight to the rented vehicle used in that lady's hit-and-run. The FBI is happy, because the same suspect has now confessed to offenses in several states – he's attempting to cut some sort of plea-bargain deal, but I don't know how much good this is going to do him. There are several organizations that neither you nor I should know about who are also happy, for reasons which they either won't tell me, or I'm not at liberty to discuss. And a general wave of unbridled good will seems to be sweeping the planet at the moment on your behalf.'

His voice was very dry. 'It's slightly bizarre. People who normally couldn't be bothered to give other people the time of day are asking us to be lenient with you.' Winters sat back and looked at them. 'Frankly, I think they're misunderstanding exactly *what* you did, in some cases, or *why* you did it, in other cases . . . but, still, some of them have a point.'

Leif stole a glance at Megan. She was holding very still. 'All of this being the case,' Winters said, 'I really doubt if sacrificing you on the altar of blind obedience is going to do anyone any good. I would just as soon leave the option open that, some day, you might possibly serve with the – what's the phrase I heard used? "Grownups?" '

Megan squirmed. So did Leif. 'Do you read minds?' Megan said abruptly.

Winters looked at her and raised an eyebrow, then said, 'Not usually. It makes my head hurt. Faces are more than sufficient. As for the rest of it—'

Winters raised his eyebrows, pushed back in his chair, pushed the report away from him a little bit. 'Something you are going to have to understand, should you come to work with the "grownups," should you eventually reach that beatific state yourself – is that your work as part of a team is not necessarily about being "right" – and there is a very, very small gap between being "right" and being "righteous." The latter state can be fatal. The distance between the two is enough to get you killed, or your partner killed, or some innocent person around you killed.' He looked over at Megan. 'What if your father had come down in the middle of that, a few days ago? What if one of your brothers had stumbled into it?'

Megan was staring at the floor again, her face burning. 'All right,' Winters said. 'I'm not going to belabor the point. You seem at least vaguely conscious of the implications. But at the same time, the question also applies to you.' He turned to Leif. 'You were next on the list. He had the address of your school. He would have found you there. He would either have tried to take you away, and possibly succeeded – in which case we would have found you in a ditch somewhere, or a river – or he would have tried to deal with you on the spot. There are any number of ways he could have done it, and any number of ways he could have killed one of your schoolmates "accidentally" at the same time. Responsibility,' Winters said. 'It would have been yours.'

Leif, too, became very interested in the carpet. 'Some day it *may* be you,' Winters said. 'All I can offer you, at the moment, is how this feels right now: this shame, this guilt, this fear. All I can do is tell you that this is infinitely better than what you will feel when, because of your disobeying an order, one of your mates goes down in the line of duty. A death with no meaning, or something worse than death.'

The room was very still. 'Speaking of which,' Winters said, sitting forward a little again. 'Your friend Ellen—'

'Elblai! How is she?' Megan said.

'She woke up this morning,' Winters said. 'She's been told what's going on – she insisted on being told, apparently. They say she's going to be all right. But she's apparently extremely annoyed about some battle that she missed with this—' He leaned toward the desk, looked at another of the papers in the stack. 'This "Argath" person. Who, by the way, turns out to be completely uninvolved in all of this.'

'We thought so,' Leif said.

'Yes, you did. Which was interesting, considering how little hard data you had to go on. But hunches come into our line of work, as well as hardware . . . and riding the hunch on the short rein is definitely a talent we can use.'

Winters sighed. 'All right, you two. I'm not going to throw you out of the Explorers, as much because I hate to waste valuable raw material as anything else. I emphasize the word "raw." '

He looked at them both, and they both looked at the carpet again, faces hot. But Leif looked up. 'Thank you.'

'Yes,' Megan said.

'As for the rest of it – if in the near future we find a piece of business which is suited to your unique talents of nosiness, inability to take "no" for an answer, annoying persistence, and screwy thinking . . .' He smiled. 'You'll be the first to hear about it from me. Now go away and compose yourselves for the press conference. Both of you have the grace to conduct yourself like modest little Net Force Explorers, or by God I'll—' He sighed. 'Never mind. See what you do to me? A whole morning's worth of composure shot. Go on, get out of here.'

They stood up. 'And before you go,' Winters said, 'just this. There's nothing more fatal than believing a lie is the truth. Think of all the fatal lies you just saved the world from. Even with all the other things you got wrong, and did wrong . . . that's something you can be proud of.'

They turned and went out, flashing each other just the quickest grin . . . though being careful not to let Winters see it.

'Oh, and one last thing.'

They paused in the dilating doorway, looked over their shoulders.

Winters was shaking his head. '*What the heck is a "Balk the Screw?"*'

. . . Elsewhere, in a room with no windows, three Suits sat and looked at one another.

'It didn't work,' said the man who sat at the head of the table.

'It did work,' said another of the men, trying not to sound too desperate. 'It was only a matter of a few more days. The first announcement impacted the company's stock more and more severely as the media

208

spread the news of the first attack around. A few more hours, the next couple of attacks, the next announcements, would have affected their stock so drastically that they would have had to stop trading. People would have deserted that environment in droves. But more important: the technology worked.'

'It worked *once*,' said the man at the head of the table. 'They know about it, now. It had to work and *not be found*. It's a *cause célèbre*, now. Everybody who's heard about this is going to be going through their databases, looking for evidence of non-presence or surrogacy among their users. This was a tremendous window of opportunity . . . but now it's shut.'

Silence fell in the room. 'Well,' said the man who had tried not to sound desperate, and failed, 'the necessary paperwork will be on your desk in the morning.'

'Don't wait till the morning. Have it there in an hour. Clear your desk, and get out. If you go now, I'll have an excuse when Tokagawa gets here in the morning.'

The third man in the suit got up and went away in great haste.

'So now what?' said the second man.

The first one shrugged. 'We try another way,' he said. 'It's a shame. This one had possibilities. But it's made some suggestions for other possible routes of attack.'

'Still . . . it's a shame we lost this one. Wars could have been fought inside a paradigm like this. Real wars . . .'

'But only as real as the controlling software makes them,' said the first man, with the slightest, chilliest smile. 'What we've proven is that the present technology is insufficient to what we have in mind . . . not secure enough to convince our customers to use them instead of more conventional battlefields. That's not necessarily a bad thing, though, because the assumption would be that when the next wave of technology comes along, it'll be watertight. And of course it won't be. We'll be there again, building in the "back doors." And from the beginning of the process, this time, rather than starting in the middle. Because of this failure, we'll be smarter. And those of us who aren't smarter, will be cleaning out their desks . . .' He looked at the second man. 'And where will you be?'

'If you'll excuse me,' the second man said, rising to leave, 'I have a phone call to make.'

When he was gone, the first man sat and thought. *Oh, well. Next time . . . for what man has devised, man can unravel and debase, and at any game, there's always a way to cheat, if you look hard enough.*

Next time for sure . . .

At the very edge of Sarxos, the legends said, was a secret place. It had many names, but the one which was most frequently used was the shortest. It was the House of Rod.

Some Sarxonians, standing on the uttermost heights of the northeastern mountains of the North Continent, and looking westward in the clearest weather, claimed to have seen it there: a single island, a mighty mountain peak standing lone in the wild waters, far out in the Sunset Sea. Tales of the place abounded, though you were unlikely ever to meet anyone who had ever been there. The souls of the good departed went there, some of the stories said, and dwelt in bliss with Rod forever; other stories said that Rod Himself went there, on weekends, and looked out on the world that he had made, and found it good.

Few knew the truth of any of these stories . . . But Megan and Leif knew, now.

It was a castle. That was more or less unavoidable. But there the resemblance stopped, for the place looked like it had been designed by an Angeleño architect who had had a bad dream about Schloss Neuschwanstein, and tried to execute a copy of it in a cross between Early Assyrian and Late Rococo. Green lawns were laid out around it, with tasteful flowerbeds full of asphodel. There was a small white beach where you could land a boat. It was said that the Elves liked to stop there, on their way into the West. 'The True West, though,' Rod said, amused. 'This is the *Fake* West. You want the *true* one, you keep going the way you're going, straight off the planet, hang a right at the second moon, and straight after that, you can't miss it . . .'

From the main body of the castle, one tall tower speared upward, with a balcony looking east. All the castle's windows looked east. All Sarxos lay there, the cloud-capped mountains and the seas, the lakes, the distant glint of clouds reflecting back the sunset . . .

'Nice view, isn't it?' asked a voice behind Megan.

She turned around and nodded at Rod, who was holding a can of cola and looking out the window past her. 'We get great sunsets here,' he said, 'but you can only see them from the tower.'

'Personal reasons?' Megan said.

Rod looked resigned. 'To the architect, maybe. My ex-wife called it a "feature." I call it a nuisance. I think she just wanted to make sure I got plenty of exercise.'

'Is it a long way up?'

'The traditional number of steps,' Rod said, 'three hundred and thirty-three. That's why I put in the elevator.' He grinned.

Megan laughed, turning to look at all the people gathered in the first-floor room. Nobody refused an invitation to a party like this, if they could help it – and who would want to help it? There were a lot of the "departed" around, players who had died in one way or another during gameplay, and every player who had ever been bounced. Shel Lookbehind was standing not far from the buffet table, happily discussing third-world reconstruction with Alla. There was Elblai, chatting amiably with Argath, whom she had never previously met in the flesh; 'I'm just the *honorary* dear departed,' she was saying cheerfully, 'and believe me, I don't mind . . .' And some of the fortunate living of Sarxos were there too . . . Some people weren't exactly clear why Megan and Leif were there, but weren't inclined to pry. Some – Sarxos support staff, or friends of Rod's – knew, or had a clue, and were keeping their mouths shut. 'I can't go too public about it,' Rod had said to Leif and Megan earlier. 'You know why. There are people who'll twitch. But all the same . . . I wanted to say thanks.'

Now Megan wandered over to the far side of her room, where her dad and mom were standing with drinks in hand, talking animatedly with Leif's mom and dad. As she came up, Megan's mother looked around them with a smile that was not as grim as it might have been, considering the talk that the two of them had had the day before. 'So *this* is what it's all about, honey . . .'

'Maybe not all, Mom. But . . . these are the people we were helping.'

'Well . . .' Megan's mother rubbed the top of her daughter's head, an affectionate gesture which immediately caused Megan to try to smooth her hair back down into some semblance of order. 'I guess you did good . . .'

'More than that,' Elblai said, coming up behind Megan with her niece, both of them smiling at Megan. 'I wanted to thank you again for what you did. It's rare enough that people just reach out to people, to try to help . . .'

'I had to,' Megan said. 'We both had to.' She looked over at Leif, in a desperate attempt to get some help with this embarrassing situation.

He stood there and nodded.

'You should be very proud of your daughter,' Elblai said, and Ellen's niece said to Megan, 'I'm still feeling so stupid that I didn't believe you that night. If I had, it could have saved so much trouble . . .'

'You were playing by the rules,' Megan said. 'It's just

the way it goes. The Rules take care of themselves . . .'

'True enough,' Elblai said. 'Have you had some of those little sushi, the omelette things? They're really good . . .'

'Omelette things?' Megan's father said, gave her an approving look, and headed off for the buffet table.

She went after him. 'Daddy—'

'Hmm?'

'*What are you writing right now?*'

He smiled. 'It's a history of the spice trade. Couldn't you tell?'

'You are not! You're making it up!'

'Of course I am. I have to get revenge on you somehow.' He grinned. 'Listen, Megan. I'm glad that what you were doing Thursday night really was important. Otherwise we would have had words. But after this, anything so important that it's likely to get you shot at . . . I claim the responsibility to hear about it first. Okay?' The look he turned on her was both annoyed, and profoundly concerned, so that she found it impossible to be annoyed with him.

'Uh, yeah. Yeah, Dad.'

'Good. Meanwhile, you can read what I'm doing when it's done. Next week sometime.' He turned away, smiling. 'Learning patience is good for you.'

'I'm going to hack into your machine . . .'

'You're welcome to try,' he said with an evil grin, and went off to investigate the omelettes.

Megan headed off to where Leif was standing, looking out the window. 'Want to go up the tower?'

'Sure, everybody else has been up there by now . . .'

They made for the elevator. At the top of its run, it came out on a small, circular room with no apparent support between it and the pointed candle-snuffer roof on top. The last of the sunset was dying away westward: to the east, over Sarxos, the moon was coming up fat and full. The second moon came up off to one side, in the 'passing lane,' as it were, and crept steadily past the first one, heading upwards fast across the sky.

Far away, the moonlight glinted on the snows of the northeastern mountains. Above them, in the sky, the stars started to go off like fireworks.

There were *oohs* and *aahs* from downstairs. 'Hey,' said a casual voice from way down the stairwell, 'they're *my* stars . . . I can blow them up if I want to. They grow back in the morning, anyway . . .'

Far eastward, a winged shape came soaring. It grew bigger, and bigger, and impossibly bigger. 'What *is* that?' Megan said.

Leif shook his head, and stared.

It came on, the huge shape, closer and closer, its great blackwebbed wings like thunderclouds against the darkening night. Right past the tower it banked, looking at them, an experience like being looked at by a low-space transport. The wind of its passing was a storm.

Those huge wings spread in a stall, flapped. The wind got worse for a moment, then settled as the king-basilisk lowered itself carefully to the peak of the mountain on which the House of Rod was built, made sure of its grip, and folded its wings down. It wrapped its long slender tail around the mountain top, for extra grip, and leaned its twenty-foot-long head right down to gaze thoughtfully at Leif and Megan out of suncore eyes.

Down in the water, a sea monster put its head up on its long slender neck, followed by the requisite multiple loops, and bellowed defiance at the interloper. Lost in astonishment and admiration, Megan and Leif could only stare from one to the other.

'Welcome to my world,' said the voice of Rod behind them, 'where cheaters never prosper . . .'

This time, Megan thought . . . and held her peace.